LOKI'S WARRIOR MATE

GODS AND MONSTERS FATED MATES

REBEKAH R. GANIERE

Loki's Warrior Mate © 2021 Rebekah R. Ganiere

ISBN: 978-1-63300-098-8
ISBN: 978-1-63300-099-5

Cover art by VWZDesigns

DEDICATION

For all those who root for the Antihero, like me.

NEWSLETTER

To claim your Two FREE Books and find out more about Rebekah R. Ganiere and her other Upcoming Releases You can Go Here:
www.RebekahGaniere.com/Newsletter

All things pertaining to the Norse God, as well as Norse Mythology, are spelled in the Norse or Olde Norse way. You may notice a few words spelled differently in this series to align with the worldbuilding of the series.

- ***Hel*** - Daughter of Loki, but also ruler of Helheim. Therefore, in this series, hell is known as hel.
- ***Helborn*** - Those created by Hel to serve her.
- ***Helmarked*** - Those who have died and now reside in Helheim.
- ***Jötunn*** - A mythical Norse creature often known for being an ice or fire giant or troll. Used as a derogatory term.
- ***Yggdrasil*** — The World Tree connecting the Nine Realms. It is now the gateway that pulls all different realms together since Ragnarok shattered the Bifrost and caused rifts across the realms.

The Æsir (the main warrior-tribe of gods, who lived in Asgard)

• **Odin (Óðinn)** — Allfather; god of wisdom, war, death, and divine frenzy. King of the gods.

• **Frigg** — goddess of marriage, motherhood, the household, and prophecy. Queen of Asgard.

• **Thor (Þórr)** — god of thunder, lightning, storms, strength, and the protection of mankind. Wields Mjölnir.

• **Tyr (Týr)** — god of war, justice, law, oaths. Lost his hand binding Fenrir.

• **Baldur (Baldr)** — god of light, beauty, joy, purity, and innocence. The most beloved of the gods.

• **Hödr (Höðr)** — Baldr's blind brother; associated with winter and darkness. Tricked into killing Baldr by Loki.

• **Heimdall (Heimdallr)** — watchman of the gods; guardian of the Bifröst. God of foresight, vigilance, and beginnings. • **Vidarr (Víðarr)** — god of vengeance, silence.

• **Vali (Váli)** — god of vengeance; born specifically to avenge Baldr by killing Höðr.

• **Hermódr (Hermóðr)** — messenger of the gods; rode to Helheim to try to ransom Baldr.

• **Loki** — the trickster god, shape-shifter, sky-traveler, and mischief-maker. Of giant blood but counted among the Æsir.

• **Freyr** — god of fertility, prosperity, sunshine, peace.

• **Freya (Freyja)** — goddess of love, beauty, sex, fertility, gold, seiðr (magic).

Loki's children:

• **Hel** — goddess of death; rules the realm of Hel.

• **Fenrir** — monstrous wolf, prophesied to kill Odin at Ragnarök.

• **Jörmungandr (the Midgard Serpent)** — sea-serpent that encircles the world.

• **Sleipnir** — Odin's eight-legged horse son (born when Loki shape-shifted into a mare)

Other Norse Immortals:

• **The Norns (Urðr, Verðandi, Skuld)** — three fate-weavers who tend the well at the roots of Yggdrasil.

• **The Valkyries** — Odin's army and those who carry fallen warriors to Valhalla.

- **The Einherjar** — slain warriors who feast and train in Valhalla until Ragnarök.

CHAPTER ONE

"I can't believe I let you talk me into this."

Loki rolled his eyes. "I think it's your mother you have to thank. I simply asked if you would go with me because I have someone I need to meet, and I don't want to get roped into conversations with others looking for free legal advice."

Thor threw him a daggered gaze. "You mean a meeting you happened to mention in my mother's presence, which happened to be on the same night as her monthly masquerade feast?"

Loki chuckled and straightened his shirt cuffs. "Wrong again, my boy. Your mother set up the meeting. It's not my fault you're so nosy you eavesdropped on the conversation and got tangled up in her little scheme to marry you off."

He wasn't about to tell Thor that the conversation he'd had with Frigg had been prearranged to try to lure Thor into going to the masquerade. The morning before the conversation, Loki had been awakened by his cellphone. He hadn't needed to look at it to know it was Frigg.

He'd had a dream involving Thor, a woman, and the masquerade. And if he'd had a dream about Thor meeting a woman, there was absolutely no doubt Frigg had as well. So, he'd answered his phone and set up a time and place for the meeting where Frigg knew Thor would be. And here they were, one week later, Loki playing babysitter and making sure Thor went to the party like he was supposed to.

Loki delved into Thor's thoughts for a moment, listening to him grumble about it being a waste of time for him to go.

He set his hand on Thor's shoulder. "It won't be any different if you don't give it a chance."

Thor shrugged off Loki's touch. "I hate it when you do that. Reading minds is creepy."

Loki shrugged. "I wouldn't need to if you opened your mouth and spoke more. You used to be so talkative. Couldn't stop talking as I remember. Mostly about yourself. Your conquests, victories, virtues, anything about you. But now-"

"Now I know better." Thor grabbed his leather coat and threw it on.

Loki checked his hair in the mirror. "I was going to say, now you're boring."

"And what about you?" Thor questioned. "I don't see you rushing out to find someone."

A permanent relationship was the last thing Loki wanted. He'd been married. And he'd had kids. Now he was content to sample all the Nine Realms had to offer.

Loki flashed him a winning smile. "I don't need to. My bed is constantly filled with whomever I find companionable for the night. No strings. No expectations. Just fun. The way I like it."

Thor walked to the edge of his loft and took the stairs down to his shop floor, two at a time. Bikes lined the walls of the solid brick structure. Thor stopped by one of the bikes.

"No time for fiddling with that," said Loki. "I still don't know why you mess with those things when you can fly."

"What about you and your squashed, brightly colored cars? You can fly, why do you drive those things?"

"Touché." Loki inclined his head.

"Besides," said Thor. "I like taking them apart and rebuilding them the way I want them. Gives me something to focus on."

Thor headed over and picked up Mjölnir.

"My car is out front." Loki pulled his key fob from his pocket and headed to the exit.

"I can make my own way there." Thor lifted his hammer to the sky and, as always, disappeared in a flash of light.

Loki shook his head. What was the fun of being in Helheim if you stuck to doing things the way you always had?

Loki exited the building and smiled at his metallic lime green Lamborghini. He owned over a dozen cars, but the Lambo was for sure his favorite. And when he took it down to the demon street races, he couldn't help but win. Which was exactly what he intended to do right after he got Frigg's most recent refugees their papers.

VAL SCANNED THE BEAUTIFUL, EXPANSIVE GROUNDS OF THE mansion, where people milled about.

"Are you sure this is where Lady Frigg said we were to meet Loki?" Elle asked.

Yup. Val glanced through the gold gates, then at the paper in her hand again, before showing it to Elle.

Lady Frigg's mansion was all the paper said, and it was pretty hard to miss her mansion in Helheim. Especially the giant ornate metal gates.

Val sighed. What was Loki up to? Or Frigg, for that matter? A party? Really?

"Come on," said Val. "Let's get this over with, and then we can go back to Midgard."

Elle nodded. Val led her across the green and past a marble fountain to the colored-glass front doors. Greenery and vines snaked up the front of the building. Standing near the entrance, a wide-shouldered, cobalt blue-skinned male nodded at people as they entered.

Val assessed him as they approached and flexed her wrists, making sure her wrist blades still worked. Not that they wouldn't. She always needed to check, though, just in case…

She strode up the cream marble steps toward the entrance, and the scent morphed into something spicy and warm. Cinnamon mixed with cognac. It made her relax a fraction as she breathed it in, before she tensed and growled.

Great. Frigg put something in the air to make people relax. Well, to hel with that. Not happening. Not for her. Not here.

Though they'd been out of Surtr's realm for a month, Val had yet to let her guard down. Armed from the shoulders downward, she didn't allow herself to slack off for a moment. She spent close to 3 hours every night continuing her training before bed. And the first thing she did when she awoke each day was walk to Sutrelle's apartment door and make sure the princess remained safe.

"Stay close," said Val

A young woman with long golden braids and bright eyes glided over to them and smiled. "Hello. I'm Fulla. You must be new here."

Val recognized Frigg's handmaiden. How many Asgardians now lived in Helheim?

"I'm Val. We have a meeting-"

Fulla smiled brighter. "Of course. Lady Frigg said you would be coming." She looked at Elle. "You must be Elle."

The hairs raised on Val's neck. Something was definitely off about this meeting. Val's eyebrows smashed together. "I don't understand. We were told to be here at 8:00."

Fulla nodded. "If you will put these on and follow me, I can get you ladies a table."

Val looked from Elle to Fulla. Being in Helheim made Val twitchy. Too many prying eyes. Too many loose lips. And too many oversized ears itching for any piece of gossip to get them a leg up. Even though Helheim was its own realm within the Underworld and no one was allowed to cross the borders from other realms unless Hel said they could, it still didn't make the world safe.

Val opened her mouth to decline the masks, but Elle stepped forward.

"Thank you, Fulla." Elle handed Val the silver fox mask while she herself affixed a golden cat mask to her face. Elle grabbed Val's hand and followed Fulla toward the tables lining a red velvet curtain.

"This is strange," said Val. "Why do we need masks to get a table to talk to Loki?"

"Maybe it's a game? Or maybe it's to protect our identities? He has a lot of clients. I'm sure we aren't the only ones he is helping. Maybe he is trying to help us not be recognized. I'll get some food, and you have a drink." Elle threw Val a smile.

Val wanted to object, but before she could say anything, Elle headed for the buffet. Val scanned the room. She didn't like it, but if she played along, they were less likely to be recognized in the sea of masked faces.

She walked to a table strategically set so she could keep an eye on the ballroom.

Val's back itched between her shoulder blades, and she fought against scratching. She knew what the itch meant, and it'd been getting worse and worse lately, particularly when in Helheim.

Val glanced over to where Elle stood picking out a plate of food from the long table.

Sutrelle's body language relaxed as she perused the delicacies. But the instant she relaxed, Val became even more alert. Because the moment Sutrelle began to relax was the moment Val needed to be more vigilant than ever. Running from Surtr meant Sutrelle's death if she was caught, but Val had experienced what Surtr did to those he deemed a traitor – and death was the last thing Surtr would do to them if he caught them.

A moment passed, and Val glanced around for a bar, but it stood all the way on the other side of the expansive ballroom. Damn.

The growing crowd of people made her twitchy. She wanted to get the documents she needed and get Sutrelle back to their apartments above Frigg's bar.

Lady Frigg had taken them in and offered them shelter after running from Muspelheim, and Loki finally had the human paperwork needed to change their identities, bringing them one step closer to freedom. It irritated Val how many different pieces of identification humans needed to live on Midgard. Birth certificate, Social Security Number, Real ID? As if Midgard was afraid they'd lose people, or worse, they wanted to keep tabs on their every movement- much like Surtr had.

Living on Midgard for the last month had been… strange. The sights, smells, and noise of Los Angeles were nothing like what she was used to. And the people, especially the men, left something to be desired. On dozens of occasions, she'd been hit on, flirted with, and flat-out objectified by the human men. And in every instance, she had made each of them a bet. If they beat her in an arm-wrestling contest, she would have a drink with them. But if they lost, they would have to give her the money they would have spent on the two drinks instead. So far, she'd won over a thousand Midgardian dollars.

A hand jutted in front of Val's face, holding a flute of champagne. She tensed and looked up.

A tall, crimson-skinned man with broad, minotaur-like horns and a golden elephant mask smiled at her, revealing sharp teeth.

"Are you new here?" he asked in a deep voice tinged with an accent she couldn't place.

Val stared at the champagne but didn't take it. "New

would infer I had any desire to be here, which I don't. So, no, I'm not new here, I'm stopping by to pick something up."

His head cocked to the side, and he chuckled. "Okay."

She got the distinct impression he had no idea what she'd said. "Is this your first time here?"

He shook his heavy head. "Nope. Been coming for more years than I can count. Just hoping tonight will finally be the night."

"The night for what?" she asked.

He smiled again. "For me to find the one I am meant to be with."

And that was her cue. "Well, I hope you find her. Or him. Or... whomever."

The male continued to stand for several seconds, hand still outstretched, but when she didn't move, he snorted and walked away.

What the hel was that? Were they at a mating party?

"Hello, Val." Lady Frigg smiled and handed Val a mug of something heady. "Thank you for coming."

Val swigged the drink, the sweet taste gliding across her tongue, but making her teeth ache.

"Was this your doing or his?" Val set the mug on the table.

Frigg continued to smile. "I thought this would be a place to meet since you can be in disguise, and plus, there's food and drink. I thought it might be easier for you to relax in such an atmosphere."

Val studied Frigg. Frigg's beauty remained unaffected by age. Long strawberry waves cascaded over her shoulders and down to her waist like they always had. Beautiful emerald eyes stuck out from under thick dark lashes. She possessed a natural beauty that no makeup could enhance and a grace that Val found herself jealous of, but only as a warrior. Her genuine compassion and kindness only endeared people to her all the more. But Val was no fool. Frigg also held the mischievousness of a mother trying to get what she wanted for her family.

Val swigged her drink and looked around again. "So is he going to show up or…"

Frigg chuckled. "Loki always likes to make an entrance. He should be here any minute."

Val snorted. "Yeah... He's always been an attention whore."

Frigg cocked her head. "You know him?"

She knew him all right. She knew all about him from her Valkyrie sisters, who had taken a tumble or two in his bed. She would call him a manwhore- but there were more Norse gods who had bedded as many women as Loki than there were those who hadn't. So, how could she judge? Just because she'd never given it up to the god of mischief didn't mean she was a saint.

"I've seen him. And let's say I had a lot of sisters who... spent time with him. His reputation precedes him even larger than his ego."

Frigg burst into a tinkle of laughter, so contagious that Val almost smiled herself.

Frigg winked at Val and squeezed her shoulder. "I'm so glad you came. You really are quite perfect."

Before Val could ask her what she meant, Frigg swept away and headed toward another table.

Sigh… she had no idea what Frigg had gotten them into, but so far, she didn't like it.

As Loki strode up the steps of Frigg's mansion, several of the females waved to greet him. He smiled and continued on through the door. Thor walked straight to Loki and shoved a mask into his chest.

"What's this?" Loki inspected the mask and scowled. "You didn't."

"If I have to, you have to."

"Why? Frigg's not my mother. I didn't promise her anything."

"Payback."

"For what?" Thor opened his mouth, but Loki held up his hand. "Never mind. Fine. But I'm only doing this because if I don't, Frigg will have my balls for earrings. But don't think this is the end, cousin."

Thor snorted. They may both be Norse Gods, but they were far from being any kind of blood relation. The closest relation to Loki besides his children was Thor's adoptive mother, Frigg.

Loki sighed before affixing the snake mask to his face and looking around the tables for the person he'd come to meet. Long blonde hair and a straight ramrod spine caught his gaze. She sat at a table, perfectly positioned for defense and for a swift exit if necessary. It was the exact table he would have chosen, so it had to be her. A shiver skittered over his skin, making him want to turn around and run out the door.

"Don't tell me you're scared," asked a light voice.

Loki glanced at Frigg, who held a glint in her eye. She was

up to something, but it didn't matter. Whatever she had up her sleeve wouldn't work. He was more than happy with his life, and he intended to keep it that way.

Instead, he inclined his head, smiled, and strode for the table.

CHAPTER TWO

Val eyed every person at the masquerade and calculated their danger factor. The helborn, she could easily take on her own. The shifters would be doable as long as they didn't fight together. Vampires, meh. But the other immortals were her biggest challenge. She calculated the odds, and at worst, she should be able to hold off the entire room long enough for Elle to run.

As she scanned the beings starting to look her way, a tall figure with hair as dark as a starless night moved like a shadow into view and strode toward her with the air of a man who knew everyone watched him, yet was above them all. And there was only one being she knew of who could possibly be that arrogant.

In one seamless motion, he slid out the chair opposite her and took a seat. His gaze, sharp and bright like a flash of lightning, stayed locked on her face the entire time. A playful grin curled his lips, promising pleasure and mischief. He wore a deep navy suit, paired with an open white shirt showing enough to flirt with formality. The golden snake mask twisted around his features in a seductive dance. The ideal emblem for Loki, God of Mischief.

"Valkyrie?"

Val glanced around to see if anyone heard him, but everyone appeared otherwise occupied.

She nodded.

He studied her, his gaze raking over her face and body as if imagining what she looked like under her clothes.

She forced her breathing to stay even under his scrutiny and took in every nuance of his expression, which told her he appreciated what he saw.

After a minute, he waved his fingers and a bottle of wine, along with two full glasses, appeared on the table. He reached for his glass, pulled the deep burgundy liquid to his lips, and sipped it- still watching her, as if trying to decide whether to bed her- or bed her.

"Do you have the papers?" she finally asked.

His eyes widened. He snapped his fingers, and a thick envelope appeared in his hand. He pushed it across the table and set down his glass of wine.

Val grabbed the envelope, opened it, and thumbed through the documents inside. She had no idea what she was looking for or whether they were correct, but she checked them out anyway.

"They're all there," said Loki.

She nodded and continued to inspect the documents.

"You know, Val really is a silly name. You should be more careful."

She looked up at him. "Thanks for your concern, but I can take care of myself."

"Elle for Sutrelle. Val. Valkyrie. Kind of on the nose, don't you think?"

She shoved the documents back in the envelope. "It's my name. It's been my name for a thousand years." That part was true. Valkyrie had been her nickname for a thousand years. But that didn't mean it had always been her name. She had another name. One given to her by her mother before being taken as a child to serve as a Valkyrie. But she wasn't about to let anyone know or use that name. It was hers and hers alone. The last piece of herself that hadn't been stripped away by the Norse gods, or by Surtr's torture.

"I simply mean, if you want to recreate yourself, don't you think a new name would help?" He twirled his glass through nimble fingers, but never let his gaze leave her face.

"Calling me by something different wouldn't change who I am, so why bother?"

He let out a silky throaty laugh, and her gut clenched as a shot of something warmed her nether regions.

No way. Absolutely not. She was not going to let the Loki, Norse god of mischief and trickery, get to her. No matter how beautiful his chiseled face. No matter how smooth the timber of his voice. No matter how much she wanted to see what he looked like underneath his crisp suit and white button-up.

"Is that it?" she asked.

Loki nodded and then cocked his head to the side, letting his long, black hair fall over his shoulder. "Have we met before?"

"In person? No."

He chuckled. "I just wonder what it is I've done in the past to make you loathe me so intensely. If we've never met, then surely I couldn't have spurned you."

Val's grip tightened on the envelope. "I don't loathe you. I don't think a thing of you."

Loki's eyes flashed for a second, and then he pressed her glass of wine across the table toward her. "It's the most expensive wine in the world. Won't you try some?"

Val pushed the glass back toward him. "I don't drink wine. Especially pretentious, excessively priced wine."

"Then how about some ridiculously cheap wine from a discount store?"

She glared at him, unable to form a response.

Loki's cool fingers brushed against hers, and an unexpected surge of longing coursed through her, heating her from within and threatening to unravel her. A sudden wave of desire settled deep between her legs, making her fear she might lose control right at the table.

Man, it had been a long, long time since she'd been laid.

Their gazes locked, sparking something electric between them. A whirlwind filled her mind as if she'd downed too much ale; suddenly, Loki seemed like the center of all things in existence. His breathing slowed, and his fingers traced lazy circles over hers.

Loki's gaze locked on hers, and her entire body buzzed. A scent surrounded her. Fruity and musky at the same time. Warm like a gentle caress. A whisper of breath tickled her neck, sending goosebumps up her skin.

Seconds passed as her body thrummed with desire, and a moan caught in her throat. Something scratched at the back of her mind as her brain screamed at her to wake up. Cold water splashed over her, and using every ounce of willpower she possessed, she ripped her hand from his grasp, dropping the envelope of documents to the floor in the process. Every sense crashed back down around her. The music of the orchestra, the scent of food and drink, and people. The bright candlelight bounced off the red and pink decorations once more.

She whipped a dagger from her boot. Rage flowed through her like the lava of Muspelheim. Her breathing came out heavy, and her heart pounded like the drums of the rock giants of Giantland.

Loki sat back in his seat, dragging her glass of wine with him and bringing it to his lips.

"Don't you ever use your illusions on me again," Val ground out between her clenched jaw. Every inch of her body went into fight or flight mode, and she fought against the urge to attack him.

Loki didn't say anything for a moment and then held up the glass in front of him. "You know, I do believe you are right. This Screaming Eagle Cabernet 1992 really isn't worth $500,000 a bottle." He waved his hand, and the wine disappeared, and two flagons of ale appeared in the wine's place. "I believe this is more to your liking. I get it straight from Valhalla. You'll enjoy it."

The way he ignored her words infuriated her. As if he was dismissing her.

"Did you hear me? Or did you want to lose something important to you?"

Loki smiled, but the smile didn't reach his eyes. "I understand why you don't like me. Back on Asgard, I probably wouldn't have liked myself either. But I'm not like that anymore… well… mostly. Now, at least, I no longer lie to women about my intentions to get them in my bed. They are all well aware I want no strings attached. But you should never date a man like me."

Val kept her mouth from falling open. How in the world could a person be so irritating? "I don't need dating advice from you. I'm more than capable of making decisions for myself, and they are not made purely with what's in my underwear."

Loki chuckled. "I can too, but it's not nearly as fun. By the way, I don't wear underwear."

He was unbelievable. She'd heard about Loki the manwhore. Loki the betrayer. Loki the trickster. But seeing him in the flesh explained so much. His good looks and charm, all mixed together with a wicked tongue and absolutely no shame. If he had been any other man, any other man, she might have considered allowing him to bring her pleasure. Sadly, he was so arrogant he probably couldn't see beyond his own pleasure to think of anyone else.

A deep-skinned man, who would have reminded Val of a fire giant had he not been so short and thin, approached the table and looked at Loki for less than a second before bowing and apologizing.

Bowing? Really? What the hel entitled Loki, a fallen Norse god, to be bowed to?

"Come now," said Loki. "Try the ale. Tell me more about yourself."

Out of the corner of her eye, Val spotted Elle rise from her table and rush out.

Val snatched up the envelope from the floor and threw him a snide smile. "I'd rather drink the wine."

The ashen-skinned man moved out of her way as she bumped the table with her hip, being sure the mug of ale tipped Loki's direction.

LOKI LEAPED FROM HIS CHAIR TO KEEP HIS ONE-OF-A-KIND Tom Ford suit from being destroyed, but at the last second, he bumped into the male who had approached the table and caught several droplets of ale on his shirt.

Damn. Imported silk was not meant to be splashed with ale.

"I'm so sorry," the Helmarked said. He dabbed at Loki's shirt with a napkin, but Loki smiled and pulled away.

"Totally my fault. Think nothing of it. Please, enjoy your evening." He headed after Val without looking backward.

She looked as fantastic from behind as she did from the front. In tight black jeans and boots, she sported a perfectly round backside with strong, shapely legs from years of fighting and training. Her golden ponytail bounced as she headed for the exit, and Loki couldn't keep from following her.

Her beauty had been undeniable the moment her photo had landed on his desk. But in person, her sharp, daggered sapphire eyes had made him unable to look away. He'd met thousands of

Valkyrie in his lifetime. And all of them beautiful. But this one… the last one still alive… she was something he'd never experienced before. The passion and fierceness radiating from her rivaled his. He knew self-preservation when he saw it. And self-preservation had been carved into every single line of her body. Most intense of all, she'd smelled of wind and wildflowers. The kind he'd only smelled in the rolling gardens of Asgard.

But surprisingly, it had been how his body responded when he'd touched her hand. He'd been so stunned, not only by seeing glimpses of what her life had held, but also by how she'd somehow called to him. Not her, but something deeper, the real Valkyrie inside the tough exterior. The one she'd locked away and never let anyone see. The creative, loving yet fierce one that he'd seen ripped from her mother's arms at a young age to start her training.

She glanced over her shoulder as she reached the exit, pulling off her mask and dropping it. His heart stopped when he caught sight of her face in person. The face of an angel with the lips of a sinner waiting for him to worship.

His pants tightened around his erection as he imagined those lips on his skin.

She spotted him, rolled her eyes, and exited.

How could she look so sexy when she wanted nothing to do with him? Dominant women had never been his style, but damn if she couldn't melt his frost giant heart.

Loki raced for the door, but didn't have to look far to find Val with her blade pointed at Thor of all people. He'd not even thought about Thor after being handed his mask.

Loki removed his mask and tossed it away as Val pulled Elle from Thor's grip.

"Hey," Thor protested. "Now wait a minute. Who are you?"

"Val," Loki interjected, strolling down the steps.

Val glowered at him, making him smile. She was good at that.

"I am more than capable of taking care of myself, thank you," she growled.

"So you've told me. Twice already," Loki replied, flashing her his best smile.

Val rolled her eyes again.

How in the world was she so immune to his charms? He'd never once given a woman that smile before, only to receive an eyeroll in return. Usually, the response involved melting, fluttering, flushing, and sometimes even throwing themselves at him. But never an eyeroll. He wondered how often she'd practiced rolling her eyes because she'd damn near perfected it.

"We should go," Val said.

"Wait." Thor grabbed Elle's hand again.

Val pulled his hand from Elle's. "No. No waiting, Odin's son. We are leaving."

Loki took a step forward, ready to defend Val if necessary. Not that she needed defending. Honestly, she might actually stab Loki for trying.

"Thank you for your kindness, Thor Odinson," said Elle.

Now that was the kind of woman Loki would have gone for in the past. Soft spoken and eager to please. But the way Elle's eyes remained downcast, and the timid way she stood, was nothing compared to the way Val's fiery spirit called to him.

Interesting...

Val tugged Elle away and headed down the street. Loki took a step to follow them, but as if knowing his intention, Val turned to him and brandished her wristblade as if flipping him off. He couldn't help but laugh. What would it be like to get her in his bed?

He held his hands up before putting them in his pockets. Didn't matter, he'd find her whether he followed them or not.

"When do you work next?" Thor called without thinking.

Elle turned over her shoulder. "I work every day."

Val said something to her, and Elle continued down the cobblestone street and into the mists beyond.

Thor stared at the spot Elle had stood moments before and rubbed his fingers together.

Oh Odin! Thor had it bad. Frigg had been right in her prediction to send Thor tonight.

Loki chuckled and slapped him on the shoulder. "Has the mighty Thor finally found a match?"

Thor eyed him. "And what about you? You seemed in unusually banterous form with Elle's friend."

Loki gritted his teeth and focused on the direction the women had gone. He didn't like that his intentions had been read by Thor. He didn't need word getting around that there was something going on between him and Val that wasn't. Or did he? If others thought Val was his, they would leave her alone. Maybe then he'd have a real shot with her.

Damn, where had that come from? He didn't want Val to be his. Did he?

"Business nothing more," he finally said.

Thor snorted and pulled Mjölnir from his jacket pocket.

"You keep telling yourself that, cousin. Are you fighting tonight?"

"Yes," said Loki. "I promised Baldur a rematch. Again."

Thor nodded. "Then I'll see you at the Throne." He raised his arm to the sky and jumped.

Loki watched Thor disappear and then looked back at the darkened street. His body yearned to go after Val. To press her against the giant windows in his house overlooking the city, and take her. To feel the length of her strong body cocooned against his. Her legs wrapped around him. Her mouth on his.

Loki shook his head. What was that? Had she bewitched him?

No. He was immune to that sort of trickery. He was trickery.

Loki growled. He didn't like the feelings bubbling inside him. Feelings of... of what he didn't quite know. All he knew was he didn't like them, and he needed to get his head right before he did something he'd regret.

Since being with Val wasn't going to happen, he'd do the next best thing to sex. The one other thing he excelled at.

He waved his hand, and his clothes changed from his suit to a kilt and a white tank top. All he wanted now was to take all his pent-up tension and confusion over Val out on Baldur.

He wondered if Baldur would ever get tired of losing to him. Didn't matter, tonight Loki wasn't going to take it easy on him. And when he was done, he was going to try something he'd not done in a thousand years. He was going to try to dreamwalk into Val's dreams.

Loki clapped Baldur on the back as he pulled him to his feet. "This makes what? The two thousandth time you've tried to pay me back for what happened so long ago, I don't even remember?"

"You tricked my brother Hödr into killing me."

Loki chuckled. "Oh yeah. That's what it was. What does it matter now, though? We're all here in Helheim together."

Baldur growled. "Exactly."

Loki handed Baldur a towel for his bloody nose and walked him to the edge of the ring. "Come on, Baldur. You were the favorite. Everyone loved you. You were so damned annoying. And it was a joke gone wrong. I really didn't think Hödr could make that shot, you know, being blind and all."

"A joke? I died." Baldur's eyes flickered with anger.

Loki sighed. "Yes, you did. And every time we step into the cage, and you try to make me pay for what I did, you are the one who is really paying. Reliving it all over again. I don't see Hödr in here trying to kick my ass every month. Why don't you let it go? Move on. Find a woman. Settle down. Have chubby, cute babies and just… live?"

Baldur stared at Loki, and for a minute, Loki thought he might take the advice. Instead, Baldur shoved the towel into Loki's chest and stormed off. Loki shook his head. He knew how it was to live in the past. To remember the old slights and quarrels, but in Helheim, all of that seemed so trivial. Thor hating Surtr. Baldur hating him. Val hating him…

He jumped to the floor and wiped the sweat from his face. Val… In the old days, whether fighting or screwing, both had given him the same high. But somehow, having gone a few rounds with Baldur barely scratched the surface of what stirred inside him for Val.

Loki grumbled and headed for one of the backrooms.

As he turned down the long stone hallway. A voice sounded behind him.

"Are you ever going to let him win?"

Loki turned to find Odin walking toward him. White hair pulled back in a ponytail. Piercing blue eyes, a leather jacket, and a ringed hand, he looked completely different from the Norse god who had once punished him by tying him to a rock and letting acid drip on him. But the aura of power still exuded from him like a golden bubble.

"What would be the point of letting him win?" Loki asked. "If I did, he would accuse me of letting him win, and then he'd get even angrier. The object is to give him a fair chance to beat me, and I always do."

Odin nodded and held out a wad of cash to Loki. Loki took the thick stack of money and folded it into his hand. "People still think he's gonna beat me after all this time?"

Odin shrugged. "You can't win every time, Loki."

Loki smiled. "Says who?"

Loki rolled his car past the ten-foot gates and into his chic, modern sanctuary of sleek white surfaces and expansive glass panels that framed a dazzling view of Los Angeles. The glow from the skyline merged with the dusky night, casting a soft, ethereal light on the driveway. He emerged from his car and flicked on his car alarm; a mere formality given the fortress-like security encasing his property: cameras surveilling every angle, imposing fencing guarding the perimeter, and ever-present, there was Loki himself.

As he ascended the broad glass staircase bordered by vibrant greenery, a gentle soundscape of trickling water from nearby fountains filled the air. Each step was flanked by planters overflowing with meticulously cared-for botanicals- white roses blushed in moonlight contrast beside ivory gardenias exhaling their delicate fragrance into the night; plush peonies stood stately among emerald carpets of ground cover. Everything appeared as it should: sharp lines intersecting with organic forms. Neatness and precision reigned supreme-how Loki preferred it.

The cool touch of polished steel railings under his fingers steadied him as he approached his personal realm. A space painted in stark monochromes and subtle hues, with its minimalistic surface. In this curated world, order wasn't merely aesthetic; it was an extension of identity, a mirror reflecting the inner harmony he craved, muting out the chaos once known only too well.

With a simple wave of his hand, the massive cream-colored front door swung open effortlessly, bypassing the need for any fingerprint scan. As he stepped inside, the tranquil notes of classical music filled the air from discreetly installed speakers in the ceiling, creating an atmosphere of elegant serenity. The coolness of the white marble foyer was tangible beneath his feet as he made his way toward the stairs, where each step on the plush cream carpeting absorbed his footfalls.

He pushed open the French doors leading to his bedroom and took in the familiar sight—a room immaculately arranged thanks to his housekeeper's meticulous touch. Everything was in its place within this realm of austerity and orderliness. Transitioning fluidly from there into his expansive bathroom: a vast walk-in shower encased in glimmering tiles and a sunken tub that invited indulgence with its promise of accommodating four people comfortably.

Reaching out, he turned the gold-plated shower handle with an ease born from habit. He peeled off his clothes, savoring every moment. Part of an unhurried ritual he'd cherished over decades. A ritual tied intimately not just to routine but also to soothing comfort at day's end.

The hot water hit his skin like a baptism of steam and heat, and he stood under the pressure of it until the tension in his shoulders finally began to loosen. He braced both hands against the cool marble wall and let his head drop forward, water cascading down the back of his neck, over the sharp ridges of his spine.

She was still in his head.

He scrubbed his hands over his face and turned the water off. Wrapped a towel around his hips and padded across the heated floor to the decanter on the sideboard. He poured two fingers of a single malt Scotch- one of the finer things the century had produced- and walked to the floor-to-ceiling window overlooking the city below.

Los Angeles glittered. Neon and shadow. Vintage stone dressed in electric light. And out there, in one of the cramped apartments above the Raven Weaver, Val was- what? Sharpening her blades? Checking locks on the doors and windows? Standing over Elle and watching her sleep with that fierce, quiet vigilance she wore like second armor?

He gulped his drink.

The towel dropped when he turned from the window, and he didn't bother to retrieve it. He moved to the edge of the enormous white bed. Pristine. Every pillow and fold of linen immaculate, because he rarely slept in it. He didn't need much sleep. But as he stood looking, he found his imagination doing something entirely without his permission.

He saw her there.

Val. Stretched across the white sheets like a warrior goddess who had finally let her guard down. Golden hair spilled across the pillow. That long body bare and luminous against the white, every line of her—supple and strong and achingly real. Those sharp sapphire eyes, half-lidded and dark with wanting, fixed on him. Her lips parted. Her voice low and stripped of all its practiced indifference as she called his name.

Loki.

He exhaled through his nose and growled.

He'd imagined women before. Thousands of them over thousands of years. It had never felt like this. Like a hook behind the sternum. Like something that mattered beyond the mechanics of desire.

What infuriated him most- and he was self-aware enough to admit it- was that she was immune to him. Completely. Wholly. Infuriatingly. He had turned his smile on her, the one that had unraveled queens and shieldmaidens and sorceresses alike, and she had rolled her eyes. Rolled them. As though he were a tedious inconvenience rather than the most dangerous and compelling creature she was ever likely to meet.

Was she awake?

He tried to picture it. Val standing, bare feet on cold floorboards, blade in hand, running through forms in the dark, the way soldiers did when sleep wouldn't come. Or maybe she was already in bed, flat on her back in the way of someone who had learned to sleep still, economical, ready to move in an instant.

Was she dreaming?

And if she was- was it of him?

He almost laughed at himself. Almost.

The empty glass dissolved from his fingers.

He lay back against the white linens and stared at the ceiling. The city hummed below, distant and inconsequential. He hadn't dreamwalked in what? A thousand years, give or take a century. He hadn't had reason to. Hadn't wanted to. The last time he'd slipped through the membrane of someone else's dreaming mind, it had been a different age, a different world.

But Val remained rooted in his head, and he wanted to know why, because she had no business being there in the first place.

He closed his eyes.

He let the city noise fall away, layer by layer, the way one peeled bark from a birch. The distant thrum of bass from some club. The honk of a horn miles away. The hiss of the air conditioner. He let it all go until nothing remained but the dark behind his eyelids and the slow, deliberate rhythm of his own breath.

Her face.

He built it carefully. The architecture of her. Those cutting sapphire eyes, sharp as a blade's first edge, the kind of eyes that looked at a man and saw straight through to the part of him he kept bricked up and mortared. The line of her jaw. Strong and clean. The slight flare of her nose when she was angry, which had been- he smiled faintly- essentially the entire time he'd known her. The full, wicked curve of her mouth that said things her words never did.

Her voice. Low and unhurried and without deference.

I would never think of you.

Liar. He smiled again. Of course, she would think of him. Whether she wanted to or not, he would make sure of it.

Her lips.

He lingered longer than necessary, but he was nothing if not thorough.

The breath moved out of him in one long, slow release, and he stopped fighting the pull and let himself go under.

The twilight between waking and sleeping was a place that had no color of its own. It shifted and morphed and smelled different every time. It was nothing and everything all at the same time. Tonight it smelled of cold stone and something faintly floral- wildflowers, he realized, and his chest tightened with recognition. He moved through the grey membrane of it the way he walked through water, not swimming, more like being carried by a current that knew where it was going even when he didn't.

He had forgotten how strange and uncomfortable it was to give up complete control and let the world take him where he needed to be.

The panic hit him before the light did. It was the helplessness of it. The not knowing. The being carried somewhere unknown rather than choosing. He nearly wrenched himself back by sheer instinct alone. His chest seized. Every muscle in his body went taut with the need to grab control of something, anything, and he had to force himself to breathe through it the way he'd once forced himself to breathe through the acid. Through the chains. Through every moment in his long and complicated life, when he'd been at the mercy of something larger than himself.

Let go, he told himself. *Let go.*

And then the grey dissolved, and light shone through.

Warm, golden, unfiltered sunlight poured down from a sky so blue it hurt to look at, and he stood at the edge of a forest he didn't recognize, with the smell of wildflowers so thick and sweet it almost suffocated him. The field stretched out before him in every direction, rolling and unhurried, full of color-lavender and white and soft yellow, bending in a breeze carrying the faint, distant sound of steel cutting air.

He went absolutely still.

She moved through the field the way water moved through stone- finding every line of least resistance, every crack and crevice, and filling it. Her sword caught the light in long arcing flashes as she worked through her forms. She wore almost nothing. A top, torn at the hem and the shoulders, leaving her stomach and arms bare to the sun, the fabric doing little to conceal the muscled lines of her torso. The breeches cut ragged above the knee, ripped for range rather than modesty, and she had none. Every step, every pivot, every controlled extension of her blade was a study in pure power.

He watched. He hadn't intended to. He'd told himself this was reconnaissance. Curiosity. A simple matter of understanding what it was about this particular woman that had lodged itself beneath his skin. But he watched, and he forgot to be strategic about it.

Her footwork was impeccable. She never telegraphed a movement before it happened, never let her weight shift prematurely, never wasted a single motion. She was economy and devastation all at once, and when she finally opened her wings-

He exhaled.

They were enormous. Broader than he remembered from the old days, from the battlefield, from the beautiful and terrible sight of a Valkyrie in full flight. They caught the air and lifted her with an ease that made it look effortless, and in the sky she was no less precise than she'd been on the ground. She carved through the blue above him in long, banking arcs, the sword a bright streak at the end of her arm, her body turning and dropping and rising again like something born for this. Like the sky had been made for her rather than the other way around.

He watched until she folded back to earth without a sound, the grass bending under her feet, the wings tucking closed behind her.

He stepped out of the trees.

It was instantaneous. One moment she was in motion, and the next completely still, facing him with the sword leveled at his chest and her eyes fixed on his face with an expression that was not afraid, not startled, just- ready. The point of the blade as steady as the ground beneath them.

"Who are you?"

Her voice was exactly the same. Low, unhurried, stripped of any invitation.

"No one," he said.

She studied him. The sword didn't waver. Her eyes moved instead, tracking his face with a precision that made him feel like a map being read.

"You're familiar to me."

"I have one of those faces."

She didn't buy it, but she didn't press it either, which told him how her mind worked: she filed the information away rather than confronting it. Tactical. Even here, even in this sun-soaked dreaming field, she was tactical.

"Do you want to spar?" he asked.

She laughed. Not a polite laugh. A real one- short, bright, and amused- it speared him in the gut like a thrown blade.

"I'm a Valkyrie," she said. "I train officers." She tilted her head. "I've been doing it for two hundred years."

"That's impressive."

"It is," she agreed, without any false modesty. "So do you think you can beat me, or are you just bored?"

He considered the question with the gravity it deserved, which was none.

"Want to bet?"

Her eyes sharpened. "What kind of bet?"

"If I win," he said, "you give me a kiss."

A pause. The breeze moved through the wildflowers between them.

"And if I win?"

"Whatever you want."

She lowered the sword a fraction. Not in concession- in consideration. She turned it over, looking for the angle, the trick, the catch. He kept his expression open and easy and gave her nothing to find.

"Deal," she said.

"What do you want? If you win."

Her chin lifted. "That's my secret." A beat. "Do you want to back out?"

"Absolutely not."

He pulled his blades from the air, the two short swords that manifested by his own magic, blue-edged and luminous in the daylight. Her eyes tracked them, then moved back to his face, recalibrating.

She raised her sword and came at him fast. Faster than he'd braced for even knowing what she was. The first exchange was brief and rang out across the field with a sharp metallic crash, ending with both of them stepping back a pace after the testing. She attacked again, no hesitation, no circling, just a clean and committed strike that he deflected, redirected, and turned into a half-spin, which put him behind her for half a second before she wheeled and drove him back with three strikes in rapid succession.

He grinned. He couldn't help it. She was extraordinary.

He parried, slipped, and countered. He kept it light, easy, genuinely enjoying himself. He couldn't remember the last time fighting had felt like play. Even the bouts with Baldur were obligation in motion. But this- following her, reading her, staying one breath ahead- was the most fun he'd had in longer than he could calculate. Not only that, sparring with her told him more about who she was than weeks of talking ever would.

She noticed his relaxed nature.

He saw it happen. The moment she registered he wasn't struggling, something shifted in her expression. Her jaw set. Her strikes came faster, harder, less fluid, and more insistent.

He smiled again, though he tried not to. Anger was sexy on her. It made her cheeks flush and her mouth purse in the most adorable way.

The tempo climbed. She stopped holding back and came at him with everything. Suddenly, he had to actually work, had to move his feet and engage properly. The field rang with the sound of steel on steel as the wildflowers swayed around them, and the sunlight caught the edges of their blades. Her wings flared for balance when he pushed her back, and he used the distraction to change the angle of his attack, which she recovered from in half the time it should have taken.

She was furious and magnificent.

She came at him in a rush, all restraint gone, her body wholly committed, and he stepped into it rather than away from it, let the collision happen, and for one suspended second they pressed together- his forearm against hers, her shoulder against his chest, both of them locked and straining- and the heat of her skin real. Even in the dreaming the warmth of her radiated through the torn fabric of her top, and her breath came hard and fast against his jaw. Her eyes loomed so close he caught every shade of blue layered inside them.

She shoved away.

He let her.

She came again, faster, and this time he dropped his weight, swept her feet, and took her down with him into the wildflowers, rolling once before he pinned her, his hips bracketing hers, one hand catching her sword wrist against the ground, the other braced beside her head. Both of his blades dissolved in the grass.

They both breathed hard.

Her eyes blazed, but not with anger.

In that moment, he couldn't hold back, and he kissed her.

He'd told himself he wouldn't, that it was just a bet and the bet was enough. But feeling her breath on his face and smelling the scent of her musky and sweet did something to him.

Her mouth was warm and real, and she tasted like honey and something wilder. He forgot every measured intention he'd arrived with as his hand moved from the ground to her jaw, her hair, then down the line of her throat to the bare skin of her waist, tracing the hard, smooth curve of her where the torn fabric ended. She made a sound against his mouth that undid him.

Then she bucked hard, and the ground came up to meet his back. She'd used his distraction against him with a hip roll that flipped their positions, and before he'd fully processed the sky above him, cold steel pressed at his throat. She straddled him, her thighs locked around his hips, her chest still heaving, her hair loose around her face, and her eyes not angry but something else.

"You were only supposed to get a kiss if you won," she said, her voice and sword hand steady. But her cheeks remained flushed, and she hadn't moved off him, and that told him everything.

"You're right." He didn't attempt to shift the blade or her. "I apologize."

She stared at him.

He held her gaze and kept still, which took tremendous effort, because she was warm and solid above him, and her hair hung over one shoulder, and she smelled of wildflowers and steel and something indefinably her. He fought to remember why restraint was supposed to be a virtue.

"So." He kept his voice even. "What do you want?"

She looked at him for a long moment. The sword stayed at

his throat. The breeze moved through the flowers around them. Somewhere above, a bird called once and went quiet.

She leaned in close to his ear and licked up the side of his throat, making his pants suddenly much too tight.

"That's my secret," she whispered. She bit his neck and then sat up.

Her expression fell, and anger flashed across her face.

"Loki."

He opened his mouth, but the dreamworld cracked.

It happened the way dawn happened- not all at once, but in a spreading, irreversible bleed of light at the edges. The wildflowers lost their color first, bleeding to grey and then to nothing, and the warmth of the sun went with them, and the weight of her above him dissolved.

He reached for her. Instinctively. Stupidly. But she sifted through his fingers like smoke.

Loki opened his eyes to the white ceiling of his bedroom and lay still for several seconds, listening to the hum of the air conditioning and the sound of his own pulse.

His erection fought the cool air as if still reaching for Val as well.

He blew out a breath and groaned, throwing his hands over his face. That had not gone as expected… Now he was even more pent up.

CHAPTER THREE

"Take these to table one." Val slopped three steins of beer on the tray in front of Elle and pointed to the table before returning to the shelf behind the bar and grabbing a bottle of rum. She couldn't help her foul mood. All she'd done was go to pick up some damn papers from Loki, and not only had he gotten her all flustered and bothered, but then she'd dreamed of him all night like some lovesick temple virgin. What the hel was that?

Never once had a man- or god- turned her into an aching bitch in heat. And she'd be damned if she'd let Loki of all beings do it. The god known for chewing women up and spitting them back where he'd found them. Too many of her sister Valkyries had told her stories of how he'd wooed them for a week or two, taking them into his bed and showing them the best time of their lives, only then to move on.

But she couldn't blame him alone. Her Valkyrie sisters had

heard the stories about him. Knew his history. They hadn't gone into it blind. But still…

Elle lifted the tray and headed to the table as Heimdall caught Val's eye. He held up his stein, she nodded, and grabbed him a new one. Heimdall had quickly become a surprising comfort to her. Sitting in the corner, day in and day out. Watching every mortal and supernatural who came into the bar. Keeping a closer eye on everyone else who ventured through the portal from Helheim to Midgard. His all-seeing golden eyes let Val relax enough to do her job without worrying about Elle every second. Heimdall knew who they both were. Knew their pasts. Knew everything about them, and yet he kept his mouth shut, as he did for every other being. Val appreciated that about him. Always had. The fact that he knew everything about everyone and yet never gossiped or judged. He simply did his job and accepted everyone for who they were. Despite that, she didn't believe he would let something happen to them if he could help it.

Elle returned to the counter. Val caught the slight glow that tinged the edges of Elle's irises.

"Elle." Val grabbed her shoulder.

Elle's head jerked up, and the glow faded. She wondered if Elle even realized what had happened. Val had seen the magic Elle held deep inside. Knew how dangerous it could be. Unleashing her power in any way could alert anyone to their presence. Not to mention the havoc it would cause in Midgard. Humans didn't know the first thing about magic, immortals, or Helheim. And everyone was happy to keep them ignorant.

Val pushed a stein toward Elle and jerked her chin toward

the corner. Elle gave a tight smile and headed toward Heimdall's table. Val tracked her. Elle and Heimdall spoke for a moment, and then Heimdall did something Val had never seen before. He touched Elle's hand. Val's mouth fell open, but her gaze hardened as Thor walked up to the table.

Shit. Why was he there? In their month on Midgard, he'd not once come up to the topside of Frigg's bar, and now they'd seen him twice in less than twenty-four hours.

The last thing Elle needed was Thor Odinson sniffing around and finding out who Elle was. Who knew what the god of thunder would do when he found out Elle was the daughter of his mortal enemy.

"Hey, sexy? Can I get a beer?"

Val glanced to her left. A man with hair like wheat and a body like Magic Mike staring at her with a smile meant to melt panties. His penetrating dark eyes watched her with the intensity of a predator. If he hadn't been so damn good to look at, she would have told him where to shove his 'hey sexy'.

"Hey," she said. "What brand?"

His smile widened. "What's good?"

She shrugged. "The house ale is decent."

"Only decent? I was looking for something a bit better than that."

Flirting? Yeah, she could use some flirting from someone like him after the dreams she'd had about Loki.

"Unfortunately, we don't serve anything amazing until after closing." Why did she say that? Stupid question. She knew why. She hadn't been with a man since before Muspelheim, and she was due for a good time.

He chuckled, and his eyes hinted with an inner glow. “When’s closing?”

A shifter, but more than that, an Alpha. He should be a hel of a good time. “Weekdays at one a.m. and weekends at three.”

“So tonight, at say, one thirty, I can try something amazing here?”

Val chuckled. “Maybe.”

“I’m Marek.”

She nodded. “Val.”

“Short for Valerie?”

“No, Valkyrie,” she said without thinking. Dammit. She needed to keep it together. How the hel could she be so stupid? She’d just been so stressed about Thor finding out who they were, and here she was blurting it out.

“Valkyrie? Like the Norse warrior chicks. Very cool.”

Elle approached the bar, and Val poured the hot shifter an ale before walking over.

"What's wrong?" Val asked.

"Uh... nothing." Elle bit her thumb.

Val scanned Elle. Her skin had a rosy sheen, and she chewed her nails like they were potato chips. "Why are you flushed?"

"Am I?" Elle touched her cheek.

Val eyed her. "You're chewing your fingers again."

Elle dropped her hand and looked away. "I need another beer."

"Which table?"

"Heimdall."

"He never drinks more than one an hour."

"It's not for him." Elle continued not to meet Val's eye.

Val glanced over Elle's shoulder. Thor had seated himself at Heimdall's table and seemed in deep conversation. "Elle-"

"I didn't ask him to come."

"We've talked about this. If he finds out who you are-"

"Lady Frigg knows. And Heimdall and Loki-"

"But Frigg, Heimdall, and Loki didn't try to kill your father. And thousands of fire giants. And vow to kill them all after Ragnarök." She looked around. "And though most of these are mortals, any number of sups pass through here who, I am sure, would be more than happy to sell you out for money or favor with Surtr."

"Then why did we run? Why did we come here if I'm still going to spend the rest of my immortal life looking over my shoulder? I might as well have stayed and let Thadren have his way with me. At least with him I would've been protected."

In many ways, Elle was still so sheltered. She'd been through a hel of a childhood, but she had no real idea what could happen to her.

A waitress approached with an order, and Elle stepped to the side. Val grabbed the ingredients and started mixing the drink.

She crushed a lemon and leaned in to Elle. "You are protected. I will protect you. I just want you to be careful."

"I'll do my best. But I can't ask him not to come to his mother's establishment. That would be more suspicious than if I do nothing."

"Then continue to do nothing. Don't be discourteous, but don't encourage him either. If Thor Odinson finds out who you are, you can bet he will want one of two things: to use you to hurt Surtr, or to kill you to hurt Surtr."

Elle snorted. "Too bad he doesn't realize my father would have killed me himself if he'd cared enough about me to lift a finger."

When Elle escaped with Val, she'd anticipated her life getting easier, not harder. She shook her head. She should have known better.

"Problem?" Frigg appeared next to Elle and smiled. "What can I do to help?"

Val gave Frigg a tight smile. "Nope." She grabbed the mug and dumped it out, then wiped down the counter with a towel.

A table of men caught Val's attention, and she nodded. "Table six wants you."

"But… the beer-"

"I'll take it," said Frigg.

Elle nodded and headed off.

"I know you are worried about her, but you don't need to be. She is perfectly safe with all of us."

"Is she?" Val's gaze returned to Thor.

Frigg grabbed Val's hand and squeezed it. The contact soothed and warmed Val at the same time. Frigg had always had that effect on people. Her kind, motherly nature, soft voice, and eyes couldn't help but make people comfortable. Even so, Val had seen Frigg fight and knew firsthand how formidable Frigg's magic could be.

"Val, you need to relax. I know you haven't been able to for years and years, but you need to. Take a day off. Have some fun. Remember who you are. Find out who you want to be."

Val's gaze slid to the shifter who sipped his beer.

"I don't know how to relax anymore."

"Then maybe it's time someone helped you remember."

Val looked back at Frigg.

Val poured Thor another beer and handed it to Frigg. "Did you send us to meet Loki at your house on purpose last night so Elle could meet Thor?"

Frigg winked, squeezed Val's hand, and walked away, but stopped and looked over her shoulder and stared at the back of Marek's head for a good ten seconds before blinking several times and turning and hurrying to Heimdall's table.

Val frowned. What was that about?

Suddenly, Marek sniffed the air and looked around in confusion. Then his gaze landed on Val again, and he smiled and asked for another beer.

Loki sat at his oversized desk staring out his office window when his cellphone rang. He didn't move for a moment as he continued to replay his dreamwalk from the night before. He'd never experienced something so real. And Val… damn. The woman had left him with the biggest hard-on since he'd woken up; it had been painful to even stand to go to work. Especially since he was still sore all over from the latest round of fighting Baldur. It surprised him he'd been able to dreamwalk at all with the injuries he'd sustained. Baldur had lost, but Loki's game had been off due to the meeting with Val.

The phone rang twice more before he picked it up without looking at the screen.

"Odinson, how interesting to hear from you twice in two days."

"I need your help," Thor said.

Loki smiled. Help? Really? That intrigued him.

"Well, well, well. I can't remember the last time the Mighty Thor, son of Odin, needed my help. Oh, wait, yes, I can. It was when-"

"Are you going to help me or not?"

Loki paused. Thor wasn't in a jesting mood. He never was anymore, sadly. "Of course, cousin. What do you need?"

"Meet me at Frigg's."

"When?"

"Topside. Now."

Loki thought for a moment. Val worked at Frigg's. Maybe he'd run into her if he went. Loki scowled. Why was the Valkyrie so damned tempting? He'd never had another female get under his skin the way she did. And he didn't even know her.

"All right," Loki finally said.

Thor hung up before Loki could say more. He set his phone back on his desk and looked at his watch. It was after the lunch crowd and before the nightly rush. Going to Frigg's and helping Thor shouldn't take up too much of his time. Besides, doing a favor for Thor would mean Thor owed him, and he could think of several things to ask for in return. All in all, helping Thor might put Loki ahead.

Loki stood and adjusted his once again erect crotch. How was it that the mere idea of seeing Val got him hard? Loki sat back down and picked up his phone to call Thor and say he wasn't coming, but stopped.

Enough. His body would just have to chill out. He wouldn't let a woman dictate what he did or where he went. Especially a Valkyrie. If he wanted to help Thor, he would help Thor, and his erection would have to go back to sleep. And there were only two ways to get it to go away. Screw something or remember the most bizarre and painful experience of his life- giving birth to Sleipnir, his eight-legged horse son. And as there was no one readily available for screwing so…

Loki placed his hands on his desk and took a deep breath before letting the memory wash over him. "I hate this memory."

CHAPTER FOUR

"Let me get this right..." said Loki. "You, Thor, God of Thunder, want me, Loki, God of Mischief, to distract a bartender so you can talk to a girl. This is why you called me all the way up here?"

"No, I called you up here because I want you to touch Elle and tell me all about her, and then tell me what you see the possibilities of the future to be. But you won't."

No, he wouldn't. Frigg had made him vow to never divulge anything about Elle, and he was not about to break a vow to Frigg- not for Thor, not even for Odin if he'd asked. Frigg was the closest of all the gods to family, aside from his children. And she'd been as close to a motherly, sisterly figure to him as anyone had. His own mother had abandoned him as a child. *Jötunn* weren't known to be overly maternal to begin with. And of all beings in Asgard and the nine realms, the one person he felt loyalty to was Frigg.

Besides, he had a feeling that if he did tell Thor, Val would kick his ass after Frigg killed him. And while she might be fun to spar with, he didn't want to have his ass handed to him by a female.

"Sorry. I made a promise," Loki said.

Thor clenched his jaw.

"Am I the only one who can't know, or are there others as well?"

Loki shrugged. "I'm not one to gossip."

Thor snorted.

"Is our business concluded?" Loki asked.

Sitting in the booth and having Val in the same room, no matter how far away, had him on edge. He'd managed to calm his crotch for the time being, but it was only a matter of hours before it would want to be used.

"Oh, please," said Thor. "Don't act like this was such an inconvenient trip for you. You had to do what? Focus on the pub for five seconds before you were able to transport here?"

"Do you have any idea what my time is worth? What I charge per hour?"

"Well, this won't take an hour. She gets her fifteen-minute break in less than five minutes," said Thor.

"After I sit here, it will have been half an hour, which equals-"

"One bottle of Odin's reserve ale," Thor blurted.

Loki stopped speaking. Odin's ale? That was the one thing even Loki couldn't get or reproduce at will. It was specific to Odin alone, and only Odin could produce it when he wanted it.

"Agreed," said Thor.

"Not so fast." Loki held up a hand. Yes, he wanted the ale,

but he hadn't wasted his time on a bottle of ale, no matter how amazing. "I agree on the ale, but you will also owe me a favor."

"What favor?"

Loki smiled. "I'll tell you when the time comes."

"That's not a deal I would agree to if I were you," said Heimdall.

Loki glared at Heimdall, who didn't appear to notice.

"You'd better decide fast," said Loki. "Your girl took off her apron and is headed for the stairs."

Thor looked over his shoulder. Elle had almost reached the bottom step. At the same time, Val finished wiping down the bar and threw the towel in the sink. She said something to the other bartender and jumped over the bar.

Damn, she looked hot doing that.

"Looks like Val is heading that direction too," Loki prodded.

"Deal." Thor jumped from the table and headed for the stairs.

Loki slid from the booth and bowed. "Heimdall."

Heimdall nodded to Loki.

Loki wound through the tables and stepped out in front of Val as she came around a pillar.

"Val, fancy meeting you here." Loki smiled and smoothed his tie.

In her black tank top and pants, she looked like a commando Barbie. Arms bare and fit, breasts round and perky underneath her tank, it took everything inside him to keep from grabbing her, pinning her to the pillar, and kissing her into submission.

Val glanced toward the bar before looking back at Loki. “Did you need something?”

Loki took a step forward and ran his finger down her arm. The goosebumps that pebbled her skin made him smile.

“Just wondering how you slept last night.”

Her eyes narrowed, and she folded her arms over her breasts before raising an eyebrow. "Fine. You?”

He grinned. “Like a baby.”

She nodded. “So, lots of crying and fear of being alone?”

Loki chuckled. He liked her sharp tongue. He could think of several things he would love for her tongue to do to him.

She tried to step around him, but he sidestepped, forcing her to continue to engage him.

“In case you didn’t notice, this is my break, so if you need anything else, you should look for a hostess on duty.”

“You’re on a break? Perfect. How about we go somewhere to continue our conversation from last night?”

“We had a meeting. You gave me what I needed. Business concluded.”

“Yes, but now that I think of it, I never did get paid. Perhaps we could discuss payment over a bottle of… whatever you want?”

Val rolled her eyes. “If you have a bill, you know where to find me.”

Loki’s courage wavered for a minute, rattling him. She rattled him. Why? He wanted to know why. Needed to know why.

“What?” she demanded.

“What, what?” he asked.

“You. The way you're staring at me.”

"Am I?" He wondered what she'd seen on his face.

Val rolled her eyes. "I don't have the time or patience for games. I've got-" She looked at the clock. "Another twelve minutes for my break, and I'd like to take them in peace if you don't mind."

"Of course not. Where are we going?"

Val growled. "You are so irritating."

"So are you."

"Is he bothering you, Val?" asked a deep voice.

Loki barely bothered to look over at the strapping male exuding Alpha aura standing to his right. The man's golden colored eyes made Loki smile, and his anger spiked. A shifter? That could be a fun fight.

"Nope," said Val. "He was just leaving."

Loki's smile broadened. She had an admirer. Wasn't that interesting? Not that he had assumed she wouldn't. Val was smokin' hot, and you'd have to be deaf, dumb, and blind not to be into her.

"I can help with that," said the stranger.

Loki laughed and finally turned to the man. "Oh, I doubt it, but I welcome you to try."

In the moment he turned, Val dodged to the left around him and raced up the stairs.

Loki looked the man up and down and then inclined his head. "Another time perhaps." He flicked a card between his fingers, which held the address to Odin's place, and handed it to the man before following Val. "Ask for me at the door, and we can continue the conversation."

"Elle!" Val couldn't help the edge in her voice. She'd thought Loki might truly be interested in her, but to see Thor with Elle made her blood boil at the thought that he'd been doing no more than trying to distract her. The thought bothered her more than it should. Honestly, it shouldn't bother her at all.

Elle flinched and moved out of Thor's grasp.

Val leaped forward and flicked her wrist blade from its sheath. "Get away from her."

Thor didn't move. "We were talking."

Val moved her blade to his throat, and again, he didn't move.

"Val." Elle stepped forward. "Val, please stop. Lord Thor was saying he was glad I made it home safe last night."

Val looked between Thor and Elle. How many freaking times did she have to tell Elle to stay away from the man? What did she have to do to make Elle see the danger she was putting them both in?

"Val, I said stop," Elle's voice came out so strong that it took Val aback.

For the first time, when Val looked at Elle, she saw Elle's mother. Her fiery eyes. Her strong voice. Head held high, demanding quiet respect.

A dull ache radiated through Val's chest. The pain of seeing her old friend shine through Elle brought with it a sense of loss that Val hadn't felt in a long while. Val sheathed her blade in its wrist compartment, gave a small nod, and took a step away.

"Why don't you let me buy you a drink?" Loki appeared at the top of the stairs.

Val scowled. "In your dreams, Playboy."

Since she wasn't going to be able to stop Elle from talking to Thor, she stomped to the next apartment down the hallway and stepped inside before slamming the door. Tears flooded Val's eyes as memories of her friend filled her. Elle's mother's laugh. Her compassion. Her strength despite everything she'd been put through. She couldn't remember the last time she'd been held by someone. Smiled with someone. Laughed with someone.

Frigg's words floated back to her. "Maybe it's time someone helps you remember."

Her mind went to Loki. She shook her head. No. Not Loki. Why would her mind go straight to Loki? No… Marek. Yes. Marek could help her remember how to have fun… and maybe more.

She looked at her wall clock. She had five more minutes. That would have to wait until later.

Val stripped off her clothes and walked naked to the shower, turned it on, and stepped under the spray before it had warmed. She couldn't stand how the smell of Midgard clung to her. Every day, she showered during her breaks. Sometimes two or three times a day. She'd wash as many times as she needed, to scrub off everything she'd been through until she could get the layers peeled away and she return to who she truly was… if she could ever find that person again.

Maybe with Marek's help, she would.

Val went through the rest of her shift with only a few bumps in the road. Thor showed up about five to pick up Elle for a date. Val had been about to tell Elle she couldn't go when Thor surprised her by stepping in to defend Elle against a table of human assholes. He even gave her the same advice Val had given a million times. Telling Elle to stand straight and raise her head to instill confidence. Val couldn't help but be a tad grateful to the god of thunder for his assistance. Just a tad.

Finally, she decided that maybe with him teaching Elle to stand up for herself, she would actually listen. So in the end, she'd stayed silent and let Elle leave with Thor without a word. Not that she didn't worry, but if there was anyone in Helheim who would keep Elle safe, it was Thor, the god of thunder.

As one a.m. rolled around, Val rang the bell above the bar signaling last rounds. Slowly, the crowd thinned, and by one thirty, as she closed the door, a somewhat familiar frame stepped up to the entrance.

"Hey there."

Val looked into the same dark chocolate colored eyes and smiled. "Hey, yourself."

"You ready to let me try that amazing thing you had to show me?"

Val nodded and ushered Marek inside.

"Wow, it's so different in here when it's quiet," he mused.

"Yeah. It's a relief when I finally close the doors at night." She locked the door and turned over the open sign.

"Do you not like working here?" Marek pulled out a stool.

"It's a job." She put away the last of the glasses and made sure everything had been put in its place before turning back to him.

"So, give me something amazing," he said.

She smiled. That comment alone could go so many different directions. "Tell me your tastes. Do you want something spicy, sweet, mellow, smooth, or holy hel firewater?"

He grinned from ear to ear and pushed his hand through his wavy hair. "I don't know if I'm ready for holy-hellfire-water. Why don't we start out easy? Something smooth or mellow."

"Okay." Val reached for one of the bottles of Pappy Van Winkle Frigg kept under the counter for the high-spending customers. She placed two whiskey glasses on the bar and dropped in a ball of ice before pouring them both a drink.

Marek held his glass up to hers and clinked it before sipping. She waited, watching him. His eyes closed as he held the amber liquid in his mouth for a moment before swallowing.

Marek opened his eyes and nodded. "That's nice."

Val smiled and sipped her own glass.

"I can see why you don't pull this out during the day for those rich college boys. They could afford it-"

"But they wouldn't appreciate it," she finished. "I was sure you would, though."

"Is that the fifteen-year reserve, the twenty-year reserve, or the twenty-three-year reserve?" came a voice from the corner.

Val's gut clenched. She swung her gaze over at the stairs leading down to the portal, where Loki leaned against the wall. His white shirt was open almost to his navel, and his blue suit coat was slung over his shoulder.

Why did he have to look so damn tempting while being utterly annoying?

Val capped the bottle and set it back under the bar.

"Not so fast." Loki approached them, his dress shoes clicking on the hardwood floor. He pulled out the stool next to Marek and sat. "I'll take one of those."

"I'm pretty sure this was a private party, friend," said Marek.

Loki flashed him a smile that didn't meet his eyes. "Private, meaning two? Or, does private mean the relatives of the bar owner are invited as well?"

Marek looked between Val and Loki and stood. "I'll let you two work this out." He gulped down the rest of his bourbon, slapped a large bill on the counter, and took a step away from the bar.

"Wait," said Val. "That's it? That's all you wanted?"

Marek's gaze went to Loki again and then back to her. "Nope. But it's all good. I'm patient. I'll see you again, Val, for Valkyrie." With a small wave, Marek unlocked the front door and disappeared out into the night.

Val wanted to run after him, to tell him to come back and have another drink… but something stopped her.

"So, do I get a taste of bourbon, or is there something else you'd like me to taste?"

Val's eyes slid back to Loki's smug smile.

"I'd be happy to help your face taste the bar." She threw him her best smile.

Loki clucked his tongue. "There you go again, irritating me."

"I'm irritating you? You're the one who came up here to irritate me. Is there something you wanted, or can I go to bed now?"

"I'm happy for you to go to bed," said Loki. "Want me to join you?"

Val growled and tossed the glasses in the sink. "Is it your goal to drive me insane?"

Loki's eyebrow arched. "I'll drive you to any sensation you want, lovely."

Val wrinkled her nose. "Do those lines work on women? How desperate are they?"

She stomped around the bar as far from Loki as possible and headed for the stairs. Why wouldn't he leave her alone? Her body rippled with tension at the knowledge she would not be getting any relief from Marek.

Loki appeared in front of her, and she pushed against his chest.

"I'm not in the mood for your bullshit."

"Then what are you in the mood for?" His voice came out so serious it made Val look Loki in the eyes.

Was he genuinely wanting to know? There was no reason for him to distract her this time. And he had no reason to be in the bar besides seeing her… For a moment, she contemplated telling him. Instead, she sighed and moved around him. But before she got a step away, Loki grasped her wrist and spun her around. He pinned her against the thick pillar in the middle of the barroom and pressed his body into hers.

"What are you doing?"

His face loomed closer to hers, his hair falling down over his shoulder and onto her breasts.

"What you wanted me to do."

Loki's taut body constrained her against the pillar, her shoulder blades digging into the corners and pinching her in uncomfortable places. She stared into his eyes, and they held something hungry and a bit scared.

Val's body relaxed without warning, and her heart raced as Loki traced his fingers across her cheek and down her throat to the top of her breasts.

She choked back the moan. No. She would not give in to his seductions. She refused to be used the way others had.

Loki leaned in close to her ear and breathed on her neck, making her shiver.

No. Not him. Not Loki… but… someone. She needed someone.

"I'll give you what you want," he whispered. "No strings. Just me, giving you pleasure, and you receiving it."

"And nothing for you in return," she scoffed.

He nipped at her ear. "In return, I will get the honor of giving you pleasure."

Val's breath hitched. Her body hummed with desire. Damn, she wanted that. Wanted it so bad it made her ache.

No. Not that. Him. She wanted him to do that.

"So, no sex?" She pulled his hips into hers, pressing his prominent erection hard against her core.

Loki groaned and nipped her ear again. "Only if that's how you want it."

She pushed him away. "It is."

Loki stared at her for a moment and then stepped up to her again, pressing his arousal against her. "Then I won't give it to you. Not unless you ask me for it."

Val fought the urge to kiss his soft-looking lips. To rip off his shirt and throw him on the floor and make him bring her the pleasure she craved.

"Let's go," was all she got out.

They took the stairs two at a time, and she practically sprinted to her door. He'd not even gotten the door closed before she'd kicked off her boots and unzipped her pants.

Loki rushed to her and stilled her hands. "Are you going to let me do anything? Or did you only want me to watch?"

Val stopped. "There are rules."

"Rules?" Loki smiled. "I've never been one for rules."

"You can live by my rules, or you can leave."

Loki ground his teeth together. "Your wish is my command."

Val grinned and pushed him by the shoulders, forcing him to his knees. "Yes. Yes, it is."

CHAPTER FIVE

Loki knelt before Val, forcing himself to keep his own need at bay. This was about her, and strange as it was to him, he would enjoy every moment of giving her pleasure and taking nothing for himself.

Normally, his needs were his first priority, but this time, he wanted nothing more than to sate her needs- mostly because he didn't want that shifter doing it- though he wasn't sure why seeing the Alpha with her had angered him so much.

"First rule," she said. "No talking."

He looked at her but said nothing.

She grinned and nodded. "Next, no intercourse."

He waited.

"No kissing. No staying the night. No asking for me to take care of you when it's over. And no telling anyone. And I mean anyone. Hel, I don't even want to talk about it. Got it?"

Loki nodded.

He glided his fingers into the waist of her pants, which

she'd already unzipped, and slid them down over her hips. The shiver she tried to hide as his palms skimmed over her tight rear and down the backs of her thighs made him smile.

He didn't dare meet her eye for fear she'd tell him to stop. And the last thing in the world he wanted to do was stop. He kneaded the flesh of her sculpted legs as she dropped her pants to the floor. To his surprise, she wore a simple pair of boy shorts. He'd not expected her to wear something sexy and uncomfortable, but the sight of the leg-hugging boy shorts made him hotter than if she'd been wearing a g-string. He leaned in to kiss her silky thigh, but Val grabbed his hair.

"No kissing," she said.

Loki smirked as his tongue glided over Val's skin with deliberate slowness, leaving a trail of wet heat. She shivered. His hand moved with purpose, fingers curling around the waistband of her underwear and tugging them down, revealing the trimmed golden curls that framed her glistening folds. The fabric pooled at her ankles, and he tossed it aside like an afterthought, his gaze locked on the prize before him.

Val's breath hitched as Loki's palms pressed against her inner thighs, spreading them. His tongue wasted no time, lapping at her with a hunger that bordered on animalistic. She gasped, her hands tangling in his hair, gripping tight as his tongue worked her with expert precision. Her moan was low, throaty, and filled with longing, spurring him on.

He wanted more. Needed more. The taste of her was intoxicating- sweet with a hint of musk that made his erection throb painfully against the confines of his suit pants. His fingers joined his tongue, sliding inside her with ease, and her body quivered beneath him. Val's grip on his hair tightened, pulling him closer, urging him deeper. Loki complied with a growl of satisfaction, his tongue flicking against her clit in rapid, teasing strokes while his fingers curled inside her, hitting the spot that made her thighs tremble.

The room grew thick with the scent of desire and the sounds of their breathing, hers ragged and desperate, his steady and focused. Loki's lips wrapped around her clit, sucking before flicking it with the tip of his tongue. Val's hips bucked against his face, her moans growing louder, more urgent. She tightened around his fingers, her pleasure building to a crescendo he was determined to push her over.

Val's body was a symphony of sensation- her breath quickened, her muscles clenched, and her skin flushed. Loki pressed his face deeper into her, his tongue delving into her folds with relentless intent. His fingers worked her in a rhythm that matched the licks of his tongue. Val's moans turned into gasps, her hands pulling at his hair with a desperation that thrilled him.

Her climax hit her, and her body arched off the floor as her thighs squeezed around Loki's head. He didn't stop, didn't relent, even as her body convulsed with pleasure. His tongue continued to lap at her, his fingers massaging her through the aftershocks until she collapsed back onto the floor, panting and spent.

Loki kissed her, his lips brushing against her outer folds before she pushed him away.

"I said no kissing," she murmured, her voice soft but firm.

Loki leaned back. "Sorry. I couldn't help myself."

She stared at him for a moment and then grabbed her

underwear and pulled it on. She stood, picked up her pants and boots, and headed to the bedroom.

Loki watched her go, scrambling for words. “So that’s it?”

She opened the door to her bedroom and turned. “I got what I needed. You got to help. We’re even. Night.”

“I can give it to you again.”

She looked tempted for a moment, but then shook her head. “Once was enough.”

She closed the door, leaving Loki on his knees, hard, bothered, and completely unsatisfied. He could fight every opponent in Valhalla’s Throne, including the Alpha shifter, and he’d still be more pent up than ever. There was only one thing that would relieve his ache for Val, and that was making Val his.

“Once is never going to be enough,” he said as he got to his feet and picked up his suit jacket.

He smiled. This was far from over. The game had only begun. A game he needed to win.

Val fell onto her bed, hating herself for allowing Loki to get her the release she’d desperately needed. She’d tried to envision Marek being the one to bring her pleasure, but she couldn’t. When she’d closed her eyes, all she saw was Loki’s intense stare. His infuriating smirk. His sexy, taut chest that she’d been able to glimpse when he’d entered the bar earlier. Hel, even his walk had made her want to throw herself at him. She couldn’t explain what his gait was like. Something between the way the predator stalked and the way a male model swaggered. All she knew was it was the sexiest prowl she'd ever witnessed.

She'd wanted more than anything to throw him on the floor of her apartment, rip off his pants, and ride him like a winged stallion. But she had to keep it together. Loki, the god of mischief, chewed women up and spat them out like sunflower seed hulls.

But… the way he'd looked at her while bringing her pleasure. Hungry. Needy. Blissful. Had not been something she'd expected. She didn't like it. Didn't like that he looked like he might actually feel something for her. Didn't want him to feel something for her. Didn't want either of them getting things like… feelings, and ideas, and… stuff.

Val grabbed a pillow and screamed into it. What the hel was wrong with her? She refused to be stupid. She wouldn't be fooled by him. He'd had his fun, she'd gotten her rocks off- not that she had rocks. The end. It had to be. Because there was no way, Val was going to fall for- or even grow to like- Loki.

The following afternoon, Val hadn't been at work for more than an hour when Loki arrived. Her mind and body collided. Her body craved his touch again, longer, closer, harder. But her mind screamed to keep away. What was it about him that made her so… so… unnerved?

She'd never been afraid of someone before, but the kind of fear he brought up in her was like nothing she'd experienced. She wasn't afraid of being hurt. Wasn't afraid of pain. She was afraid that he might actually open up parts of her she'd never let anyone see before.

He spotted her in an instant and sat at the bar.

Dammit.

"What can I get you?" she asked.

The glint in his eyes told her exactly what he wanted.

"This is a bar, not a bordello, sorry. And we don't have fancy wine here either." Not that he couldn't make whatever drink he wanted appear in front of him.

She picked up two glasses off the bar and put them in the sink.

"I was thinking more of steak."

"Don't have that either."

He chuckled. "I am aware. I meant I was thinking of going out for steak."

Her stomach growled. Damn, a steak sounded amazing. She'd pretty much been existing on fast food for a month. A new and not altogether unpleasant experience. Burgers were absolutely amazing- especially with barbecue sauce and fried onion strings.

She threw him a false smile. "Good for you."

She wiped down the wood, and Loki set his hand atop hers, making a shiver run through her. Stupid body. Why did it betray her like that? Just because he was good with his tongue and hands didn't mean she had to go all weak at the slightest touch… Okay. He was more than good; he was amazing. But still.

"I was hoping you would join me," he said.

Val's gaze met his, and her stomach clenched. The image of her crawling over the bar and straddling his hips floated into her mind.

She slid her hand from under his. Nope. She did not need him projecting those fantasies on her. Loki's fingers trailed down her skin, bringing back memories of her orgasm and making her flush.

She snatched her hand away as heat crawled up her neck. "Stop that."

He smiled. "Is that a, yes?"

"I'm… working," she stammered.

What was wrong with her? Why was that what came out of her mouth?

He reached for her hand again, but she pulled it away. "What about for your break?"

"I don't have enough time."

"After work," he persisted.

She drew her eyebrows together. "I doubt there is a place open we can get a steak at one thirty in the morning."

"There is a place-"

"Denny's? Tried it. No thanks."

A server approached the bar and placed an order. Val moved away and grabbed five wine glasses.

"No," said Loki. "Not Denny's. I wouldn't even take Fenrir there if he were in a full moon eating frenzy."

Val snorted. She'd never met Fenrir, but she'd heard of Loki's son as well. From what she'd heard, he was the complete opposite of his father. Not a ladies' man, and more animal than immortal. Feral even.

"Then where?" she asked out of curiosity.

"A place down under. You'll like it."

"You think so, do you? Because you know me so well?" Val poured the drinks and set them on a tray before signaling the waitress.

Loki touched her hand again. "Yeah. I do."

Val gritted her teeth as sensations washed over her and memories from the night before returned.

She yanked her hand away. "Why do you do that?"

His eyebrows drew together. "Do what?"

"Make me go all tingly and shit."

Loki grinned. "My touch makes you tingle? Is it just tingly on your hand or maybe-" He looked down. "Other parts as well?"

Val grabbed a paring knife and slammed it down between his fingers. "Stop." It wasn't a joke, and she wasn't playing his game.

Loki's gaze went to the knife, and when he looked back at her, his eyes had turned icy blue. He picked up the knife and twirled it between his fingers before skidding the shaft down her bare arm.

"I am happy my touch makes you tingle in embarrassing places, darling, but I can promise you it has nothing to do with any kind of spell on my part. Is it so inconceivable that what you are feeling could be between you and me?"

Val snorted. "Yes. Yes, it is."

Again, Loki's eyes flashed ice blue. He flipped the knife over and handed it to her. "Do you like irritating me on purpose, or is that a talent?"

Val took the knife and wiped it with a towel. She couldn't help being who she was. She couldn't help pushing men away. She'd never been anything but used and abused by them, so being irritating was her best form of self-protection.

"So, steak?" she said. "I like mine thick and rare."

"If that's what you want, that's what you shall have."

A pang of guilt struck her for the way she'd treated Loki.

After all, what had he done to her really? He'd flirted, taunted, followed through with no satisfaction to himself… hel, that was more than most men would do. And now he was asking to take her to dinner?

"It is," she said.

A trace of a smile whispered across his lips. "As you wish."

Elle walked down the stairs, tying her apron.

"So, meet me here at one thirty."

Loki nodded. "You're not gonna have another strange late-night visitor, are you?"

"Only you."

Loki chuckled, and she laughed.

"Wow! An actual smile and a laugh. I never knew I was so funny," said Loki.

"Technically, it was my joke."

"At my expense." His smile widened.

She couldn't argue with that.

Elle approached the bar, and her eyes met Val's.

Val dropped her smile and slapped his arm. "Get out of here."

Loki's gaze slid to Elle. "What? Are you ashamed of being seen with me?"

"Yes. Yes, I am."

Loki grabbed his chest. "Thou doth wound me to the core, M'lady."

She rolled her eyes. "Whatever."

Loki winked at her. "Don't stand me up."

She tried to think of a witty comeback, but nothing came to mind.

Loki walked to the edge of the bar and disappeared down the stairs.

Damn. How did he do that? She'd not been able to keep her eyes off him, but he'd not looked back once. Strangely, the knowledge pricked her with a tinge of disappointment.

She pushed the feeling away and turned to Elle."Take tables, three, four, and six."

Elle nodded and looked like she might say something, but she didn't. She simply picked up her tray and headed off.

It was nearly closing time when the door to the bar opened, and Marek walked in. Val's gut tightened at the sight of him. Crap. What was she going to do about him? On the one hand, she liked him. But on the other hand, she couldn't deny that something had started with Loki, and like it or not, she couldn't ignore it.

"Howdy, beautiful." Marek walked to the bar and leaned on it.

Unlike the last time he'd been flirty, something felt off.

"Hey, yourself. Can I get you something?"

"I was wondering if you were busy after work."

"I actually am. Sorry." The conflict grew inside. She wanted to go out with Marek, but she wouldn't turn down Loki for him. What did that mean?

He nodded. "Is your Norse friend showing up again?"

She wondered if Marek knew who Loki really was. She had to assume he didn't, otherwise she figured he'd never speak to her again.

"He's not my friend, but yes."

"Are you two together or something?"

Val bit her tongue at the 'no' that she'd been about to say. "Or something, I guess."

Marek's gaze grew heavy. "Is it serious?"

Val's chest tightened. She didn't like all the questions. Questions she wasn't ready to answer or even think about. Hel, she had no idea what was between her and Loki. They'd fooled around once, sort of, and now they were having dinner. Was that something? Maybe. But with Loki, you could never tell. And she wasn't ready to give up a possible chance with someone else for something that was most likely nothing. Loki was Loki after all.

"No," she finally said. "It's nothing really."

Marek smiled. "Then I still have a shot. Good. I am going to try out a new place tonight. Actually, your Norse friend suggested it. If it's good, maybe we can go there together sometime."

"If it's good."

Marek chuckled. "I can tell you're a woman who likes nice things."

Val snorted. "Trust me, I'm not one of those women. It's just that I've spent so much of my life going without or the bare minimum that I promised myself when I came here, I'd not waste my time or settle. I've done enough of that in my life."

"I like a woman who knows what she's worth and won't settle for less."

Val couldn't help but like Marek. Not only was he handsome and hunky, but he was also… nice? Was that the word? No. Easy going. His easygoing presence made her comfortable.

Which was strange because she'd never heard of a 'nice' Alpha before. It made her wonder why he didn't already have a mate.

Elle glanced her way, and Val stiffened.

"So can I pour you anything before last call?"

"Nah. Just wanted to stop by and say hi. I'll let you know if the place I go to is any good. If it is, I'll make reservations for us for Friday night. Does that work?"

Val nodded, despite the knot in her stomach.

Marek winked and tapped the counter. "Hope you have a good time tonight, but not too good."

Val chuckled. "You too."

Marek looked like he wanted to say something, but he just smiled and left.

Val watched him go, appreciating the view of his round full backside. His walk was completely different from Loki's, as was his rear. Where Loki stalked toward people like a lithe panther who would rip out your throat at a moment's notice, Marek lumbered toward people in a non-threatening, yet I'll-knock-you-on-your-ass-if-you-mess-with-me sort of way.

The moment she caught Elle watching her, Val turned to scrub the bar.

Two men. Two. Val had never even thought she'd have one man looking at her. But two was just… too much. Was it even two? Or was Loki only interested because she was another challenge? Another conquest?

She shook her head. What was she thinking? Why had she even told Loki yes to going to dinner? She stopped scrubbing and wondered if Loki had used some kind of influence magic on her. That had to be it. Every time he touched her, he did something to her.

All right then, she determined not to allow him to touch her at dinner to see if anything changed. Because if it didn't… she would be in real trouble.

CHAPTER SIX

Loki stood at the portal on the Helheim side of The Raven Weaver. He shifted the box under his arm and sucked in a breath. What was wrong with him? He'd given women gifts before. They usually gushed and then slept with him straight after, or at the very least, later. Not that that's why he gave gifts to women. He gave them gifts because he liked seeing them wear them. Especially clothing. Loki appreciated the female form and nothing pleased him more than seeing a woman he was with look her absolute best… well, almost nothing.

But this was different somehow. This time, he didn't think falling into bed with him would be Val's reaction. But when he'd seen the dress hanging in the window of a Helborn dressmaker shop. It reminded Loki of Val instantly- though he wasn't sure she would understand why.

"Are you okay?" Frigg walked up beside him.

Loki threw on a smile, but Frigg's all-knowing eyes saw through it. "Have you ever seen my future?"

Frigg smiled. "I see lots of things. Some things are specific, and some are broader in nature."

"That's not an answer."

"I see you in broad strokes. Never anything concrete."

"And what are these broad strokes?" He wasn't sure he wanted to know, but his curiosity and nerves wouldn't allow him not to ask.

Frigg smiled and squeezed Loki's arm. "I see happiness and peace."

Seriously? That's all she was going to give him?

Loki shook his head.

"You'd better go up. Val doesn't like to be kept waiting."

Loki snorted. "I wouldn't think patience was a virtue of hers." Though he wasn't patient either, so he couldn't fault her for being the same.

Loki looked at the black box tied with a satin ribbon and almost gave it to Frigg. Instead, he walked through the portal and headed up to Midgard.

Loki sat at Heimdall's table.

"Loki. What a surprise."

Loki rolled his eyes. "That joke never gets old, does it? Considering you see everything coming and going."

Heimdall shrugged. "I'd ask what you are doing here, but..."

Loki wondered how Thor could be so close to Heimdall for so many centuries. How annoying would it be to have conversations with someone who already knew what would be said?

Elle approached the table. "Would you like one more before closing?"

Heimdall shook his head. "I'm good, thanks."

Elle looked at him. "Lord Loki? Would you like anything?"

Loki chuckled. "Lord Loki? That's one I'm not used to. Thank you, Elle. I'll have a scotch."

She inclined her head and drifted toward the bar. Loki's calculating gaze followed her as she relayed his request to Val. An undercurrent of somber tension pulsed between the two women, its weight palpable even across the tavern's expanse, like a dense fog that refused to lift. Val cast a glance his way, her expression shifting through an indecipherable kaleidoscope of emotions, fleeting yet profound, leaving Loki mired in a deepening sense of anxiety.

He waved to her, and Val gave him a tight smile before fixing his drink.

Elle glanced over her shoulder at him but looked away quickly when she saw him still watching her. What a timid mouse. So strange for her to be the daughter of one of the most ruthless beings in existence, and yet so bashful that if you looked at her wrong, she might burst into tears. He wondered if that was what appealed to Thor so much. She gave Thor someone to look out for and protect, which was Thor's greatest need. To be a protector. It'd been his job for thousands of years, and in Helheim, hardly anyone needed his help.

But if Thor found out the truth about Elle's father... Lucifer help them all.

Elle brought his drink and hurried away, leaving him and Heimdall. The two stared at each other in silence while Loki sipped his drink. The last bell rang, and customers began filing out. It surprised him how awkward the air between him and Heimdall became as he waited for Val to finish up. They'd never been close. Hel, they'd never even been friends. Loki had never thought too much of it before, but he assumed it was because they had similar gifts of sight. That and the fact that Heimdall knew every single thing he'd ever done. The good, the bad, and the horrible. It was strange being around someone who knew everything about you. Like being stripped naked and inspected with a microscope. What kind of conversation could you have with someone who knew absolutely everything you'd ever done or ever would do? Especially one who remembered it all and kept it all locked away in his mind?

The thought gave Loki the shivers. There were things in his past even he didn't want to remember. Like being tied to a rock by his entrails. That... sucked rocks. No pun intended.

"Well, good talking to you, Heimdall," said Loki. "I've always said you're an amazing conversationalist. However, I think next time I'll sit alone."

Heimdall nodded. "That would be preferable."

Loki picked up his box and headed to the counter. Val locked the front door and turned over the sign as Heimdall headed down to the portal.

"Well, hello there," Loki said.

Val nodded and eyed the box. "I hope you bought yourself something nice."

"It's for you." Loki pushed the box toward her.

She pushed it right back. "Thank you, no."

A pang of irritation stung him. "Don't you want to know what it is?"

"A snake?"

Loki laughed. "Why would it be a snake?"

She shrugged. "With you, a person never knows what they are going to get."

"Have I given you any reason not to trust me?"

Conflict crossed her features, and then her face went blank. "Me? Not particularly, but-"

"You've heard about me," he paused, imagining what she'd been told, read, and seen. In the old days, he'd been with dozens of Valkyries, hundreds possibly. It would surprise him if they'd talked about how he'd used them and let them go. Or other things he'd done. After all his tricks, pranks, and vengeance were as legendary as his prowess in the bedroom. Even so… something felt… different with Val. He found himself thinking about her when she wasn't around. Wondering what she was doing or if she was thinking about him. And after being in her apartment and bringing her pleasure… it had only gotten worse. But back to the point, her distaste for him began to make sense.

"I assure you," he finally said. "My intentions are pure. Purely selfish, that is. I bought you something I wanted to see you wear."

Again, she pushed the box to him. "Sorry. I'm not into kinky lingerie."

Loki fought to keep his temper. Why did she have to be so damn... irritating? Why couldn't she accept the gift without any strings attached?

"Tell you what," he said. "You keep it. If you like it, wear it. If not, toss it. Either way, I can't return it, and no one else should wear it. It's one of a kind. Almost as if it was made for you."

She eyed the box and then tucked it under the bar. "So, about that steak."

"You still want to go?"

"I've been looking forward to it all day." She stopped, and her eyes widened. "I mean, I'm hungry, and I've not had a great steak in ages. So, I've been looking forward to having one all day."

He couldn't help the smile that spread across his lips. "Not that you've looked forward to seeing me all day?"

He waited for her quick retort. Something snappy with a tiny bite to put him in his place- but it didn't come. Interesting.

"I should shower and change," she said.

"You look great the way you are." Loki meant it. Though he preferred his women polished and perfect, somehow, with her high blonde ponytail, black tank top, and black pants, she did look like the perfect version of herself.

She scratched between her shoulder blades. "I would like to shower-"

"Nonsense. You've been waiting all day for steak."

"But..." She looked at him for a minute. "You look much too nice for me to go out with you like this."

He gestured under the bar. "I did bring you the box."

"No," she said too fast. "Thank you. I'll change and-"

Loki snapped his fingers, and his outfit changed to a pair of expensive jeans, an untucked dark button-down, and a pair of loafers. "Better?"

He could tell she wanted to fight him, but she just nodded.

"Great." Loki clasped Val's hand, guiding her around the bar. To his surprise, she didn't tug away as he led her through the shimmering portal into Helheim.

Wandering hand in hand down the steps on the Helheim side of Raven Weaver, her fingers slipped free from his grip; a subtle gesture that left a faint echo of disappointment in his chest. What was happening to him? He felt like a love-struck teenager experiencing their first crush. He'd never had to work to win over a woman before. Had never wanted to either. But for Val... Memories of her taste and scent flooded him, and he wanted nothing more than to take her back to his house and make love to her all night.

The male helborn, helmarked, and supernatural patrons' gazes lingered on them with unwarranted interest, and Loki found himself wanting to stab every leering eye. The idea of anyone looking at her ignited an irrational flicker of protectiveness within him. She was with him, and that's how it would stay. Reclaiming her hand, he steered them toward the door. No chance was he giving those smirking faces any false ideas; Val was with him. Only him. Period.

As they strolled down Helheim's dimly lit cobblestone street, flanked by quaint boutiques and mysterious emporiums, the glow from the shop windows painted an array of shadowy figures on their path. She glanced at each storefront in silence. In the witch's apothecary, jars floated eerily above herbs suspended mid-air. The bakery still buzzed with life; a handful of helborn and marked enjoyed vibrantly colored pastries that looked almost magical under the flickering lights, while the helborn behind the counter used her eight spindly arms to whisk and stir and knead and chop all at the same time.

Dark blooms crowded a florist shop, their petals seeming to thrive only in Helheim's gloom. A few smaller shops offered treasures from Midgard. A pet shop sat dark with various trained or domesticated creatures used for service or as pets. Anything and everything a place needed to try to bring back memories of lives lived before, to pass the time, or to try to gain favor with different beings in Helheim.

The crisp air tinged with a blend of ancient stonework and the underlying scent of death and suffering, while echoes of muffled laughter curled around them like wisps of smoke from further along the night-cloaked avenue.

Despite the simple act of walking together, something comforted him about the warmth radiating from their intertwined hands- the sensation whispering promises untold with every soft pulse against his skin under flickering lamplit skies.

"Have you spent much time down here?" he asked.

She shook her head. "I haven't had time. Watching over Elle and working takes up whatever time I have."

"You really do look out for her, don't you?"

"You've met her. You see how naive she is. She may have been raised in the house of monsters, but that doesn't mean she knows anything about anything."

"So, you've protected her her whole life?"

"It was her mother's dying request. Her mother was a close friend. I would have done anything for her if I could have. But Surtr..." Val trailed off.

The pain in her eyes and words was more than evident over what had happened to Elle's mother and, in turn, to Elle herself.

Loki tried to steer the conversation in a different direction. "So, you haven't been down here to explore, have you been exploring up in Midgard?"

She shrugged. "I've gone out when Elle is in bed. I don't go far, and most everything is closed, but I need to get out and walk sometimes. I hate being cooped up. It makes me..."

"Claustrophobic?"

"What?"

"Claustrophobic. It's where people are afraid of-"

She stopped and pulled her hand away. "I'm not afraid of anything."

Loki inclined his head. "My apologies, not afraid, more... uncomfortable with cramped spaces."

Val chewed her lip for a moment and nodded once.

He wondered what tortures she had been forced to endure in Surtr's kingdom. In that moment, he wanted nothing more than to find Surtr and beat him to a bloody, fiery mess. Not that he could. Even Thor hadn't been able to defeat Surtr alone during Ragnarök.

"Do you come down here often?" she asked.

Loki nodded. "Daily. I have a lot of clients in Midgard, but I also have clients here. And I like it better here."

"What kind of helmarked or helborn might need a lawyer?"

"You'd be surprised. If they want to ask my daughter Hel for a favor, they pay me to step in for negotiations and review the contract. There are times, sups get in trouble down here, and I'm asked to defend them or find out the truth. It's not serious things, but there are a lot of legalities when it comes to making contracts in Helheim, or higher up with Lucifer himself."

"Have you met him?"

"Lucifer Morningstar?"

Val nodded.

“A few times.”

“What’s he like?” Val asked.

Loki studied her for a moment, wondering why she was so curious. “Honestly? He’s a lot like me.”

She snorted.

“What’s that for?”

She rolled her eyes. “One of you is enough. I have a hard time believing the universe would make two of you.”

Loki laughed. “Oh, trust me, there is no being anywhere just like me, sweetheart. But he and I do have many similarities.”

“So he’s cocky, self-absorbed, and annoying?”

He stopped walking. Though her tone conveyed the same snarky tone it always did, for some reason, the words struck deeper than usual.

“That’s not all I am, you know.”

Her gaze found his, and she held it for a long moment while chewing the inside of her lip.

"Why do you live up on Midgard when everyone else in your family lives down here?" She changed the subject and continued walking again.

Loki let out a long breath. "Our immortal Norse family, varied and strange as they are, they and I do better when there is distance between us. Plus, Fenrir lives topside, and I like to keep an eye on him. He... struggles."

His thoughts turned to his poor son. He’d failed Fenrir for so long and in so many different ways that he did what he could to try and make up for it… Though he was pretty sure he was still failing.

"Why did Fenrir leave Valhalla?"

"He never went. After all he'd been through with Tyr and Odin and the others, he couldn't take an eternity with them as well. So, he lived here with his sister Hel. That wasn't good for him. I love Hel, but she is a bit of a handful, and Fenrir doesn't have the capacity to deal with all her drama and tantrums."

"Hel always has been one for a fight," said Val. "Valhalla knows I've had to fight against her too many times when she got the hankering for some chaos."

"She is good at stirring up chaos."

"Like her father?" Val smirked.

"That's funny. Probably true, unfortunately. But again-"

"You aren't like that anymore? Yeah, you've mentioned a few times how reformed you are now. So tell me, if you can change, why didn't Hel? I've heard how she rules her realm. Some say she is worse than Lucifer himself."

"She's not bad. She's just... who she was born to be."

He couldn't blame Val for her feelings. Hel may have been Loki's daughter, but there was no denying she was a total troublemaker. However, being the goddess of death, it wasn't her fault. She hadn't chosen that path; it had been thrust upon her. Death was her thing, which meant chaos and war were her things as well, and for the longest time, she took pleasure in her chosen job. But ever since Lucifer had allowed her to take up residence in the Underworld and given her her own little corner to govern on his behalf, she'd been relatively content. After all, Lucifer was all about luxury and the good things in life, so Hel had the dominion she'd always dreamed of. Not that that meant her subjects were content. But eternity could be much worse than Helheim, that was for sure.

The sounds of music and voices grew louder as Loki led Val

toward a brick building with glowing Edison lights on the bright marquee in front flashed the name of Odin's establishment-Valhalla's Throne. The scent of ale and perfume mixed with the scents of Helheim. The lights cut through the misty fog of the Helheim street. Valhalla's Throne occupied an entire corner of the block, its facade a deep slate-grey brick, its mortar veins iron-dark. The marquee above the entrance blazed in amber and gold, the letters casting a smear of color across the mist. Flanking the heavy double doors- black iron banded in hammered gold, engraved with interlocking knotwork- stood a pair of torches burning in shades of deep orange and ochre that threw the surrounding fog into shifting amber curtains. The bass thrum of music pulsed through the soles of Loki's shoes before they reached the door, and beneath the ale and perfume, he caught it: the metallic bite of old magic, the faint sulfur-and-cedar soaked into the mortar, into the stone, into everything that had been standing long enough to remember what it was.

Val stopped short and looked up at the glowing bulbs.

"What?"

She stared at him. "You have to be kidding, right?"

Loki looked at the building and back at her. "This is where you can get the best steak."

"Odin's place? You want me to eat at Odin's place?" The anger in her voice and eyes was enough to make Loki take pause.

Loki shook his head. "I... don't understand."

She exploded. "He's the reason all my sisters are dead. He forced us to fight everyone until finally, in Ragnarök, even though he knew what was coming, knew what had been foretold, he sent us anyway. And every single one of my sisters were slaughtered. All of them. I was the only one who remained, and the only reason I did was that I was kidnapped and put into a life of slavery."

His gut plummeted. He was losing her. "Val, I'm sorry. I didn't realize..."

She began to shake, less than a minute from cracking. In an uncharacteristic gesture, he reached out and touched her cheek. Her eyes snapped to his.

"We don't have to go here. I didn't think. I'm sorry. For me, Ragnarök was a lifetime ago, but you have had to live with its consequences ever since. I didn't realize that till now. I apologize."

She stared at him, the fire in her eyes fading somewhat.

"Let me take you somewhere else. Let's go back to the bakery. It has the most amazing deserts."

She shook her head. "I don't want to eat anymore."

Loki nodded. He didn't want it to end like this. Things had just begun to open up for them, and he didn't want to lose her to the nightmares of their past.

Loki touched her shoulder. "What do you want to do?"

She paused. "I want to punch something."

Loki smiled. "Really?"

She nodded. "I want to punch something over and over until I have no punches left."

He looked at Valhalla's Throne. "I can arrange that."

Her eyes narrowed. "I don't want to punch you. At least not at this moment."

He chuckled. "I wasn't suggesting you should. But what if I

could arrange for you to punch the very man who ruined your life and took your sisters from you?"

She eyed him. "What do you mean?"

Loki pointed to a door down a few steps on the far side of the building. "The club has amazing steaks. The basement is a different animal."

She peered at the stairs. "Show me."

LOKI LED VAL TO A SMALL STAIRWELL AND TO A THICK METAL door. Val stared at it for a moment and then followed him down the steps.

Loki knocked, and a small window slid open, revealing a bulbous brown eye.

"Password?" boomed a low voice.

Loki rolled his eyes. "Gadius, you know me. I don't need a password."

The eye looked Loki up and down.

"You could be an imposter. Password."

Loki shook his head. "*Hjaldr.*"

Battle? The password to the basement of Odin's place was battle? Fitting.

"That's last week's password." The window shut.

Loki put his hand on the door handle, and it buzzed with blue light before swinging open and revealing a low-lit hallway. The scent of stone and wet dirt drifted out.

"Hey!" said Gadius. "Wait. You got the door open. That means..."

Loki waited a moment. "It means I really am Loki?"

Gadius smiled. "Oh yeah. Hey buddy, how are you?"

Val stared at the mountainous cyclops. She had never seen one before, but he couldn't be anything else. Built like he'd been made of stone, with a giant eye in the middle of his forehead and two tusks jutting out of his lower lip, he was unmistakable. For all of his formidability, his face held a passive childlike innocence that surprised her.

Loki clapped the big guy on the shoulder. "Is Odin in there?"

Gadius nodded.

"Is the roster full tonight?"

Gadius grabbed a blank-looking clipboard off the wall and scanned it. "Nope. Just this fight tonight. You gonna challenge Odin?"

Loki looked at her. "Not me."

Val's heartbeat quickened as the cyclops gaped at her.

"Her?"

Loki nodded. "Trust me, she's a professional. She can handle him."

Gadius shrugged. "Name."

"Valkyrie," she said.

Gadius' eye widened. "Like the old Norse warrior women. Cool."

Val didn't reply. Was this really happening?

"Okay," Gadius put the clipboard back on the wall. "You're next. You know the rules?"

"I'll tell her."

Gadius nodded. "Remember, break the rules and you lose. Break them twice, and you are banned."

Val arched an eyebrow at Loki. What was he getting her into?

Loki walked her down a low-ceilinged brick hallway lined with fire-lit torches. Beneath their feet, the bricks continued down and ended at a dark velvet curtain that separated them from a noisy crowd on the other side. The torchlight caught the curtain's deep burgundy nap, and the combined heat of the flames made the low ceiling feel lower. Behind it, a wall of noise pressed through laughter, cheering, the clink of glass, at least three different languages she couldn't identify. The too stuffy, warm hallway smelled of old stone and iron. She pressed a hand to the brick wall to steady herself. She hesitated a moment. Anyone could be in there. Traitors? Mercenaries? Supernaturals willing to sell her out?

No. She had to believe Loki wouldn't put her in danger.

The velvet curtain pulsed with the muffled roar of the crowd beyond it. Loki pulled it aside, allowing bright light to flood across the hallway floor.

The smell hit her first- old blood under the bite of antiseptic, woodsmoke, and something else, something electric and ancient that pressed against her skin like static.

She glanced at Loki beside her. He stood an easy six inches taller than her five-foot-nine, lean in a way that made his clothes look architectural rather than worn. He had the kind of face that never quite settled into one expression, the blue of his eyes doing something unreadable as he watched her with mild, patient amusement. Like a man who already knew the outcome of the evening.

For a moment, she was tempted to turn and leave, but the idea of possibly being able to fight the one man she'd hated for centuries was too much for her to turn back. She had no idea if she could beat him. No idea if she'd get her ass handed to her. Either way, she had to take her shot.

They walked through the curtain into an arena of chaos. In the middle of the arena stood a cage with walls about ten feet high. Above the cage, a vaulted ceiling of rough-hewn black rock disappeared into shadow, hung with iron chandeliers that flickered unevenly, as if the flames were nervous. In the cage, two men, a demon of some sort, and a human-looking man, beat and kicked each other. All around them, on tiered stadium seating, dozens of beings sat or stood watching the fight. Yelling and cheering, they watched with great enthusiasm. The crowd was a catalog of the supernatural world crammed into one space. A cluster of olive green-skinned figures near the top row argued, their voices rattling the stone. Below them, two creatures with elongated gray limbs and too many joints leaned over the railing, their wide, oil-black eyes fixed on the fighters. The natural seating of thick logs polished to a high, dark gloss, curved in a half-circle around the cage, and the noise rolled down from every tier like a wave- roaring, stomping, the crack of someone's palm slamming the railing hard enough to split the wood. A deep-colored carpet covered the floors, possibly to hide the blood.

As she scanned the crowd, her eyes stopped. Halfway across the room on a massive wooden throne sat an older, white-haired man in a leather biker jacket. His long, wild, white wizard hair had been cropped shorter, and his unruly beard manicured into a distinguished goatee. He looked a thousand years younger than the last time she'd seen him. How was that possible?

His piercing blue eyes stayed on the fight as he sipped from a giant metal flagon. Though he looked totally different, Val couldn't miss his aura. The aura of superiority. Of disdain. Of… the king of the Norse gods- murderer of Valkyrie.

The chair-throne he sat on couldn't be missed either. Heavy, carved of wood and gilded in gold, it stood close to eight feet tall. The intricate carvings all over it depicted battle scenes from Norse mythology, as well as various members of the Norse god family. How typical of Odin. Even when his family had gotten out from under his thumb, he still sat atop them like the god he still thought himself to be. Such hubris. A thrill shot through Val at the thought of possibly being able to bring him down a peg.

Loki pulled her toward the box surrounding Odin, and her fingers twitched for her to pull one of her blades. But attacking him would most definitely earn her a death blow.

As they neared, a large gray wolf stood from where he'd been lying at Odin's feet and growled once. Three ravens took flight near the ceiling, circling them, watching everyone. They screeched above the noise of the fighters and spectators as she stopped a few feet from Odin.

Odin glanced over and smiled. "Loki. How are you, my boy? Fighting tonight?"

Funny Odin called Loki 'boy', even though Loki himself was said to be older. Then again, Odin didn't like to admit anyone was older than he was, as it might challenge his status.

"Not me. I'd like to introduce you to, or reintroduce you to, my friend, Val." Loki wrapped his arm around her waist and drew her forward.

Odin looked at her, and his expression changed. "I know you."

He remembered her? That was unexpected. They'd only met a handful of times.

He studied her for several seconds. "You're a Valkyrie," he finally said. "But all my Valkyries were killed during Ragnarök."

"Not all," she replied through gritted teeth.

Odin bowed his head for a moment. "It is good to see you, daughter. You truly are a sight to behold and bring a touch of ease to my heart. Are there more? More of your sisters who survived?"

All she could manage was, "No."

He nodded. "I'm truly sorry."

Val bit her tongue and squeezed Loki's hand hard as she was able. He glanced at her sideways and then turned his smile back to Odin.

"Are you up for a challenge?"

Odin chuckled. "I thought you said you weren't fighting tonight."

"I'm not." Loki looked at her, and Odin followed his gaze.

"You, daughter? You want to challenge me in the ring?"

Every utterance of "daughter" from Odin ignited a fiery rage within her, reinforcing her resolve to confront him. The desire to forcefully silence him by tearing out his tongue and stopping his words burned in her heart. Despite having a father she never knew and a beloved mother she was cruelly torn from to serve Odin's whims, her fury grew stronger with each passing moment.

The weight of haunting memories pressed upon her soul.

Sisters mercilessly obliterated from the worlds. The wounded, their eyes pleading for release from agony. Defiant spirits choosing to stand against the darkness, even as it consumed them. The metallic tang of blood, the putrid stench of war, the gut-wrenching scent of fear. Echoes of despair piercing the air. And the bitter sting of tears, carving rivers of sorrow down her raw face.

"Yes," Val said, the memories lending her strength.

Odin took a long swig of his ale and stared at her for a moment before nodding. "I accept."

CHAPTER SEVEN

Loki led Val to a section not far from where Odin sat watching. "The rules are simple. No magic and no weapons."

Val studied the men in the ring. The match was about to be over. The helborn had gained the upper hand, and the human-looking man struggled to stay on his feet.

"Where's the fun in that?" she asked.

"Everything here is about being fair. You need to go up against each other with only what you have. Anything else is considered an unfair advantage. Also, you need to remember this isn't a fight to the death- not that Odin can die- but still. He can't kill you. It's not allowed. Whoever ends up knocked out is the loser."

She nodded. No killing, no weapons. That didn't quite raise the stakes enough for her, but she was game if those were the rules. She may not be able to kill Odin, but she sure as hel would give him a battle. A battle he didn't even know was coming. On the occasions he'd fought alongside the Valkyrie, she had studied him at length, Thor as well. It had been the only reason she'd made it to the end of Ragnarök. And she was more than happy to show him what it would be like to fight himself.

Minutes passed, and as Val predicted, the human went down like a felled tree. Gadius walked into the cage, grabbed the man by one arm, and dragged him down the stairs before laying him on a cot to the left of the door.

She would not be dragged out like that. Being dragged out would be even more humiliating than being beaten by Odin.

"Okay," said Loki. "You're up. Are you sure you want to do this?"

"Absolutely."

Loki held out his hand. "No weapons."

Val wondered how he knew she hid a blade in her boot, but then remembered their first encounter, when she'd shown it to him... or rather, threatened him with it.

Val reached into her boot, pulled out the blade, and placed it in his palm. Loki nodded and held out his other hand.

"You really are irritating, you know that."

Loki winked at her. "So I get under your skin, too, huh?"

She reached behind her back and pulled the blade she kept strapped to her at all times between her shoulder blades.

The blade lengthened as she handed it to him, from the size of a butter knife to the full size. It's golden, immortal metal flickered off the overhead lights and shone around them. Loki slipped the sword under his jacket, and it began to shrink again.

"And the last one?" He arched an eyebrow.

Damn him.

Val reached into her pocket and pulled out a utility knife. "You really are a killjoy."

"Never been told that before. But if it saves your life, I'll take it." He nodded. "Remember the rules." He looked like he wanted to say more, instead, he touched her cheek, sending a shiver through her. "Give 'em, Hel."

She wanted to kiss him in that moment. Kiss him as they did in all those silly movies right before the hero went to risk his life. What the hel was that about? Why did she want to kiss him? She didn't. She didn't want to kiss him… right?

His eyes filled with a desire that mimicked her own.

Nope. Not happening.

Val nodded and walked toward the cage door before either of them did something she would regret.

"Val?" a low voice called.

Val's gut clenched, and she turned. Marek sat a couple of rows from where she stood. What the hel is he doing there?

Marek walked down the aisle to her. "What are you doing here?"

"I was going to ask you the same." Her gaze flicked to the cage where Odin shrugged off his leather coat and took off his rings.

He looked over her shoulder. "Your friend gave me a card with the info for this place on it. This is the place I was going to bring you on Friday if it was good."

"You were going to take me to a cage match?"

"No," he chuckled. "They serve food upstairs, but..."

She waited.

"It's a burlesque club. I didn't know, and I'm pretty sure that's not your kind of place."

She shrugged. "Trust me, I've seen enough breasts and asses in my lifetime that one is much like any other at this point. Besides, I hear they have great steaks."

Marek gave a nervous chuckle. "So... you want to come on Friday?"

"She's busy on Friday." Loki joined. "It's your turn, love."

Val glared at him.

"I think Val can decide for herself if she is busy on Friday or not," said Marek.

Loki smiled. "I would offer to take you to the ring to fight for her, but I don't see Val as the kind of woman who appreciates two men fighting over her.

"I can fight my own battles, thank you both." She couldn't believe this was happening. Here she was about to fight Odin and Marek, and Loki wanted to get in a dick-measuring match.

"How about I make it through the fight, and then we see if I'm in any shape to go anywhere on Friday. How about that?" said Val.

"Wait," said Marek. "You're fighting?"

She nodded. "I've waited longer than you can imagine for this opportunity."

His eyes flashed golden. "You could get hurt, though."

His concern touched her. Marek was so different from Loki. Loki had encouraged her, whereas she was sure Marek would have tried to talk her out of it.

Loki chuckled. "You really are a soft heart, aren't you. Val is more than capable of handling herself in or out of the ring.

She'll be fine. Besides, Odin isn't allowed to use magic or kill her, so I bet on Val to win."

Val appreciated Loki's confidence in her, but she couldn't tell whether he said it to make her feel better or meant it.

"You're fighting Odin? As in, the Odin? Norse God?" A ripple ran through Marek.

Whoa boy! Wolfing out would not be good. She was sure that would set off alarm bells and send some guards rushing in.

Marek's gaze traveled from Val to Loki and back. "Your name isn't a joke, is it? You really are a Valkyrie."

"Yes," she replied. There was no reason to lie. If he hung around long enough, he'd find out anyway; better that he learned the truth sooner rather than later. That way, he could run as far from her as possible. Someone as nice as Marek was bound to be hurt in the end. Nice guys weren't her thing anymore and hadn't been for hundreds of years.

Marek shook his head and looked to Loki. "Who are you? Thor?"

Loki sniffed. "Of course not. Thor is not half as good-looking as I am. I'm Loki."

Marek appeared as if he might pass out.

Val put her hands on his shoulders and pushed him down on the bench. "It's a lot to process, so why don't you sit here and consider whether or not you really want to take me out?"

Marek stared off.

Well... there goes one guy. Guess the measuring was over. At least she appreciated that.

Her gut twisted as she wondered when Loki would get tired of her. Dammit! Why did she keep doing that? She didn't care about Loki, or what Loki thought, or how he felt about her.

“Don’t do it,” said Marek, breaking into her thoughts.

Yup. She’d been right. Marek was trying to stop her from fighting. She looked to Loki.

He shrugged. “It’s your choice.”

As she stole a glance at the cage, Odin's eyes locked onto hers with unwavering intensity. There was no backing out. A fierce wave of anger surged through her, propelling her towards the enclosure. No backing out for her. Not for those who died. If she didn’t do it now, would she get another chance? More than that, how would she be able to live with herself if she didn’t at least try?

With a resounding thud, the door slammed shut behind her, trapping her inside the cage. Casting a fleeting look at Loki, his strained smile barely masked the tension in his posture. Was he worried about her getting hurt?

"He favors the left hook," Loki said.

She smiled as adrenaline pulsed through her. "Trust me... I know all his moves."

Several beings approached Loki, talking to him animatedly as he backed away and blew her a kiss.

She rolled her eyes. Idiot.

She had no doubt the spectators were trying to figure out who she was, what she was doing in the ring with Odin, and what her relationship was to Loki.

"Well, daughter? Are we going to do this or not?" Odin called.

Oh, they were doing it. They were definitely doing it.

Val and Odin circled each other, and out of the corner of

her eye, she caught Loki taking money from several men. A woman sauntered up to him and ran her hand down his chest, but Loki simply smiled at her, peeled her hand from his shirt, and focused on Val. A spike of jealousy rippled through her, and she wanted to rip out the woman's bright red fingernails. Jealousy? Really? Since when was she the jealous type?

In an instant of distraction, Odin seized an opportunity to strike Val. She evaded his blow and retaliated with equal force, but Odin managed to seize her fist and throw her off balance.

As Val hit the floor with a thud, she quickly regained her footing and leaped back into action, determined not to let Odin gain the upper hand again. As Val and Odin circled each other, the tension crackled in the air like static electricity. The sound of their footsteps echoed throughout the cage, creating a rhythmic beat that set the pace for the impending clash. Without a word, she lunged forward, her movements swift and calculated. Odin met her with equal aggression, their bodies colliding with a force that reverberated through the cage. A surge of adrenaline coursed through Val as she focused on anticipating Odin's next move. She evaded his incoming strike with a deft sidestep, then retaliated with a series of rapid jabs that landed squarely on Odin's chest.

His eye twitched.

Good. Now we both know where the other stands.

Odin appraised her for a moment and then attacked again, but she deflected his attack and counterattacked with one of his own moves. Odin spun around to kick her in the gut, but she'd practiced the move a million times herself, so she grabbed his foot and twisted it at the last second, being sure to kick out and catching him on the side of the knee.

Despite the odds stacked against her, Val fought on with unwavering resolve, her focus sharpening as she unleashed a flurry of strikes against Odin's defenses. Each blow landed with resounding impact as the stakes of their confrontation escalated with every passing moment.

Odin groaned and dropped to the floor. Val didn't let up. She rushed him, stomping downward on his chest. He grabbed her ankle and twisted, and she dropped beside him. She needed to get back to her feet. On the ground, his body mass would pin her.

She raised her free leg and brought it down on his face, but he grabbed the leg and shoved her away. She twisted and got to her knees, but he was up as well and wrapped his arms around her waist, dragging her back to the ground. They grappled for a minute, each trying to get the upper hand, but when he got behind her and wrapped his arm around her throat, she was in trouble.

Odin squeezed his arm around her throat, cutting off her air supply.

"There is no shame in tapping out, daughter."

She had to move fast. If she didn't, she'd pass out for sure. She grappled with his arm, but her upper body strength was nowhere near equal to his. So, she changed tactics and grabbed the back of his shirt instead. She bucked her hips into the air and flipped over his back and out of his grip. As soon as she did, she kicked him in the back and sent him sprawling onto the floor. Rage overtook her. This was her chance to show him what she could do and make him pay one thousandth of what he'd done to her sisters.

The energy in the arena crackled with tension as Val and Odin pushed each other to their limits in a relentless display of skill and determination. The audience witnessed the fierce exchange between Valkyrie and the Norse God, neither willing to back down.

As the battle raged on, Val's senses heightened, every movement honed with precision and intent as muscle memory kicked in, and she sought to overcome Odin's formidable strength and experience. The rhythm of their struggle ebbed and flowed like a dance of combat, each participant locked in a deadly embrace that left no room for mercy or hesitation.

Val's muscles screamed with exertion as she poured every ounce of her strength into each strike, pushing herself beyond physical limits in pursuit of victory, but Odin remained on his feet and unfazed, even as her strength and stamina waned. If she didn't end this soon, she was going to be pulled out just like the human from the last fight. The taste of sweat mingled with iron on her lips as she gritted her teeth in determination, refusing to yield as exhaustion threatened to overwhelm her.

She raced straight at Odin, and he ran toward her at the same time. He lunged forward, swinging at her, but she ducked, swept his leg out from under him, and sent him down. She kicked out and connected with his knee. He rolled onto his back and grabbed his leg.

She had less than ten seconds to finish him before he got back up.

Val's shoulders itched, and she did something she hadn't done in more years than she could count. She released her wings from where they hid within her skin. Her shirt ripped down the back as the tattered feathers spread wide, lifting her into the air. With all the momentum she could muster, she pushed herself downward, boots aimed for Odin's head.

"No magic," someone yelled.

"That's not magic; she was born with them," Loki replied.

A second before her boots landed on the back of Odin's neck, he rolled out of the way and hopped to his feet, balancing on his uninjured leg. Val slammed onto the ground, where Odin punched her in the gut and sent her flying backward into the cage wall. She hit the chain link with a crash and several of her feathers ripped out as she dropped to the floor, winded.

"Which of my generals taught you to fight?" Odin asked.

Val struggled to her feet, beginning to get her breath back. "You did," she spat. "Everything I learned was from watching you and Thor fight."

Odin's eyes widened, and then he paused. "You hate me, don't you? You blame me for the loss of your sisters."

"In the face of our inevitable doom at Ragnarök, you callously thrust us into battle against Surtr. The prophecy loomed over all, yet your insatiable greed eclipsed all else. You showed no regard for Thor, your own flesh and blood, or anyone else."

Val's fury erupted as she launched a left hook, the impact reverberating with a resounding crack as it connected with his jaw. Undeterred, she unleashed blow after blow, each strike fueled by a torrent of emotions. Golden blood trickled from his lip, a stark visual testament to her unyielding rage. With every punch, she expected resistance, a retaliatory strike, a defense- yet he offered none. His passivity further stoked her wrath, propelling her relentless assault.

Blow by blow, the intensity mounted. Face. Stomach. Kidneys. Ribs. Face. Stomach. Stomach. Ribs. Ribs. Ribs. Her frenzy persisted, her arms throbbing with exertion, her resolve unshakeable. She relentlessly battered him until his once-proud visage was a grotesque mask of swelling flesh and free-flowing blood, a visceral tableau of her unchecked wrath.

"Fight back! Why won't you fight back?"

Punch to the nose.

His face swelled and puffed up, but his eyes remained clear and knowing.

"Hit me!"

Punch to the jaw.

He continued to lie on the ground, immovable.

"Coward. Fight me!"

She pulled back to hit him again, but a warm hand caught her fist. She turned to Loki.

"Valkyrie," he said softly, pulling her to her feet.

"No," croaked Odin, raising to his knee. "Let her finish it."

Val didn't need to be told twice. She wrenched her arm from Loki's grip and gave Odin an uppercut to the jaw. Odin flew backward and landed sprawled on his back, eyes finally closed. Val stepped toward him, but a buzzer rang out, and Loki pulled her back.

"It's over. You won."

She turned on him. "I don't want to win, I want revenge."

Loki looked at her, his eyes conscious. "I understand, love, but even if you get the revenge you seek, it won't heal what you've been through."

"I don't need to heal."

"You do," he said. "And injuring him further won't help."

"How do you know?" she demanded.

Loki looked at Odin, who had yet to stir. "Because when we first got here, he let me take him in the ring. Odin knows what he did. We all know what we've done in the past, and we all pay for it in different ways. Just because Odin doesn't show it doesn't mean he doesn't feel all the things he did and all the lives he cost. Believe me, he pays. Every day, he pays."

Val stared down at the old god. His head moved, and he sucked in a deep breath but stopped and groaned as he grabbed his side. The door to the cage creaked, and she looked over at Gadius, who walked to Odin and pulled him to his feet.

Val glanced around at the silent crowd. She folded her wings away stiffly and stepped closer to Loki as her gaze landed on the spot where she'd left Marek.

He wasn't there.

"He left about halfway through."

That answered the question about Friday night.

She looked at Loki but didn't respond. It was for the best. She never would be what Marek hoped for anyway. She sucked in a breath but didn't let the pain show. Too many years as a Valkyrie and then in Surtr's palace had taught her what others did when they sensed weakness.

Even so, pain began creeping across her body. She would pay for the fight in many ways over the next few days.

"You okay, Boss?" Gadius helped Odin out of the ring.

Odin nodded, one arm wrapped around his ribs, the other wrapped around Gadius' shoulders. Odin stopped at the door and looked at Val and then Loki.

He spat blood on the floor. "Family dinner on Friday. I like her. Bring her."

Odin and Gadius headed between two benches and disappeared behind them. She felt she should say something, but what? Apologize? No. Thank him? That was worse. She realized her anger had begun to morph into something else. Confusion. Regret. Guilt.

"Come on," said Loki. "I'll take you somewhere you can shower and clean up."

Val snorted. "Now you'll let me shower?"

Loki grinned. "Come on, love."

He walked her to the edge of the cage, his warm hand on the small of her back where her wings had sliced through her T-shirt. The connection grounded her and gave her strength, surprising her.

She noticed none of the people who he'd been dealing with previously came up to talk to them, and she wondered what it meant. Probably, whatever they'd wagered, they'd lost.

They headed the same direction Gadius had taken Odin, and after they got behind the benches, Loki directed her to the left. They walked down a domed tunnel that reminded her of an old set of passageways they'd use on Asgard to get around unseen. The stone curved overhead in the same charcoal grey she remembered from the servant routes beneath Odin's hall-low torches guttering in iron brackets, the air close and mineral-cold against the back of her throat.

He steered her to the left and showed her to a sturdy, dark wooden door fashioned into the stone. He opened the door, and inside stood a lush, jewel-toned room. Deep teal and burgundy covered every surface: thick wool drapes pooled at the base of a narrow window, and an azure rug ran the length of the floor. The fire in the corner cast an amber glow against the stone walls, and the whole room breathed with a steady, enclosed heat, nothing like the tunnel's chill.

It was in stark contrast to the rest of the fight club, with a plush bed in one corner and an open bathroom with a shower made of glass. A fire roared in the corner next to the bed, and near the bathroom stood a wooden cabinet with a deeply carved cross on it.

A thick black phone rang on a table next to the bed.

Strange. How had phones gotten down to Helheim? What did they even connect to? But then… how did cellphones work in Helheim? Magic was the only answer she could come up with.

She limped over to the bed, her body aching in ways it hadn't for decades.

Loki answered the phone. "Hello?"

He stood near the far side of the room- lean, unhurried, one hand in the pocket of his trousers, the other holding the receiver. His dark hair hung loose below his collar, still immaculate despite everything, and his shirt hung without a single crease. Under the low amber of the fire, there was something deliberate about the way he occupied space- like a man who had never once needed to fill a doorway to make himself known.

His blue eyes moved to her briefly, then away. "No, thank you, we don't need a healer. But you might want to check in on Odin. He will say he doesn't need you, but he does."

Loki placed the phone in the cradle and walked to the bathroom. He turned on the shower head, which sprayed water like a rainstorm. Then he walked to a closet, pulled out two plush red towels, and set them on the counter. He placed a bar of soap, a toothbrush, and toothpaste there as well.

"You can clean up now."

Val looked at him, then at the shower, and back again. She wanted nothing more than to take a shower and scrub off her skin, maybe even let out her wings, but... There was no bathroom door, and the shower was see-through.

"I can get you some clothes as well. You just let me know what you want." He waited, but she didn't move. "Is there a problem?"

"You mean besides the fact that there is no door or privacy at all?"

Loki grinned. "Afraid I'll watch?"

"Only if you want a couple of black eyes." She smiled and batted her eyelashes, making her eye twitch with pain and her cheek spasm.

He snorted and walked to the bed, lay on it, and picked up a TV remote. He turned on a loud action movie and then glanced at her.

"I won't even hear you over that. And I promise to be a complete gentleman and not peek- unless you want me to." He wiggled his eyebrows.

The idea of him watching her made her skin flush. "Why are you being so nice to me?" she asked. "We may not know each other well, but you know me well enough to know that being nice isn't going to get me into your bed."

His expression grew serious, and he licked his lips as if looking for words, and then sighed. "Honestly? I don't have an answer for you. Usually, my charm and looks are enough to get women into my arms, but with you, I am honestly just trying because... it feels right. I know that makes me sound stupid, but it's the truth. I'm not trying to get you into bed, Val, though I am absolutely not opposed to the idea. I just… I don't know."

She wanted to believe him. Wanted to believe he was telling her the truth, and he really wasn't trying to play her.

He threw her a panty-melting smile. "I can tell you this, though. I've never, not ever, worked so hard to make a woman simply like me. Especially expecting nothing in return. But I truly don't want anything more from you than the joy of your company. That's it. Does that make you look at me differently? Have I lost my 'Playboy' image with you?"

Sincerity rang in his voice, making her uncomfortable. She wished he wasn't telling the truth. It would be so much easier if he only wanted to screw her. At least then she wouldn't... be starting to rethink her original impression of him. Which she didn't want to do because if she didn't hate him, if she didn't see him as a user and a womanizer, then that left her where? Open? Vulnerable? She didn't want to be either of those things. Not with him. Not with a Norse god. But...

No. No buts.

"No peeking." She stood.

He saluted her. "Wouldn't dream of it. Wait... yes. I would totally dream of it, but I won't do it for real. That I promise. What I do in my head is my own business, though."

"Is it?" she asked. "It's only your business if you keep it in your head and don't try to plant it in mine like you did the other night."

A chagrined expression crossed his face.

She knew it. She'd heard he had the power of dream walking, but she hadn't been sure until that moment. It had been him in her dream the other night. And the thing they'd done in her dream... Kissing. He'd kissed her. Her first, real kiss, even if it was only in her dreams. The idea of doing it again, mixed with the sight of him lounging on the plush bed, had her body heating up in places she didn't want.

She turned before he discerned what she thought and headed for the shower. She definitely needed a shower, and a warm one at that point wasn't necessary. She needed cold. Ice freaking cold.

CHAPTER EIGHT

Val walked out of the bathing area, wrapped in both large towels. The sight of her made Loki's body heat.

No. That's not what she needs. She's still vulnerable. She needed him to be there for her, and for the first time in his life, he was okay with that. It surprised him how okay he was with it when it came to Val. How much he took and how much he put up with. Things he would never have tolerated with another woman, or that he would have found annoying, he actually liked about her.

He pointed to the ointment and bandages that he'd pulled from the wardrobe-sized first aid cabinet. "Let me look at your injuries."

"They're fine, thanks."

Loki nodded. "I know you can take care of yourself, but I'd like to take a look. Especially your wings. They did not look like they were in good shape in the arena."

"My wings are-"

"Fine? It'd make me rest easier to see for myself. After all, I'm the one who got you into that fight."

She looked about to argue, so he stood and gestured to the bed.

"Please? Humor me."

Her eyes narrowed. "This isn't your way to get me into bed, is it?"

He sighed. "When are you going to trust me?"

She bit the inside of her cheek. "Trust isn't something that comes naturally to me. All the people I've trusted have died. I've had to learn to rely on no one but myself."

"Well then, how about if you give me one small inch of trust and sit on the bed and let me check you over. No funny stuff. We both know if I try anything, you'll pummel me like you did Odin. Here." He pulled out her blades and handed them to her. "You can stab me if I try anything."

After a brief silence, she moved towards him and sat on the bed beside him. She slipped the towel off her shoulders, letting it fall around her hips. His gaze traced the path of scars that etched stories across her skin- some deep trenches carved by fierce battles, others faded whispers of long-forgotten skirmishes. Near her spine, a jagged line told a tale of hasty stitching.

He extended his hand to trace the ridges of her past, but before he made contact, her wings unfurled with a startling grace- a sight both mesmerizing and heartrending. These were not the grand wings of legend; though they should have resembled lustrous clouds drifting lazily across a summertime sky, they were tattered remnants. Dozens of feathers lay absent from their rightful places, while those that clung on bore a muted dullness where brilliance once shone. So different from the wings she'd shown him in her dream.

A gentle rustle accompanied their hesitant movement, reminiscent of autumn leaves brushing against one another in the forest.

"When was the last time you took care of them?" he asked.

"Before Ragnarök."

"What?" Loki couldn't believe she hadn't done anything to tend to her wings in so long.

"After Ragnarök, when I was kidnapped, I had to keep them hidden. If I didn't, Surtr would try to break them. And from there we came straight to Midgard, and there aren't a lot of places to fly and stretch my wings. You know, because of all the humans without wings and stuff."

Loki reached out and stroked her wings. The feathers remained soft despite their neglect. He ran his fingers over several broken pins, and the wings twitched and trembled beneath his touch.

"Am I hurting you?"

She shook her head. "I've not had someone touch my wings in eternity."

He wondered how long it had been since she'd let someone touch any part of her. Had Surtr's men pushed themselves on her? Loki shoved the thought away before his rage took over.

"We should remove the broken quills so you can heal, and they can grow back. The broken feathers we should trim down. And then you should let me rub them with some oil to help protect and rebuild them."

To his surprise, she agreed.

He was about to ask her if she meant it, but he was afraid

that if he did, she'd change her mind. So instead, he gathered the supplies and started to work without a word.

For the next hour, he removed the broken quills from the membrane. Cut down the damaged feathers. And finally applied oil to every feather where it met the skin. Through the whole thing, Val didn't say a word; she just watched the movie on the television. When he finished, he touched her shoulders, and she folded her wings in.

"You should leave them out for the night if you can. Let them breathe a bit."

She nodded, and her eyelids drooped.

"Here." Loki walked to a closet and pulled out a pair of sweatpants and a large T-shirt. "You can put these on. I'll cut the back out so your wings have room to spread. And I'll have your clothes washed for you."

"You don't need to do that," she murmured.

He smiled at her. "I know. I'll be back in a minute. Don't leave, okay?"

She nodded.

Loki gathered her clothes, underwear, and boots, then walked out of the room. He closed the door and waited a minute, worried she might try to run for it. He'd asked her to trust him, though, so he needed to trust her in return. Besides, she was in no condition to run anywhere.

Loki strode down the tunnel to a split and turned left. He walked down another tunnel and stopped next to a large door. He knocked, and it swung inward. The scent of fresh laundry and a cloud of humidity wafted out to him.

"Put them in the basket," someone called through the steam. "When do you need them back?"

"Morning," he called.

"Will do."

Loki dropped Val's stuff into the basket as he was told, and the basket floated upward and out of sight. He turned and headed back to the room. The closer he got, the more he worried she'd taken off in his absence. But when he opened the door, she sat on the edge of the bed. She'd already cut the back of the shirt herself, and it hung loosely around her arms.

Loki closed the door.

"I should get home. Check on Elle," she said without conviction.

"Why don't you rest for a few minutes?"

She nodded and, as if she'd just been waiting for permission, lay down on her side.

Loki waited, trying to decide what to do.

"Will you stay?" she asked, not looking at him.

Hel yeah, he would. "Absolutely."

He slipped off his shoes and walked to the opposite side of the bed from Val. He sat for a moment expecting her to change her mind, jab at him, or say something else, anything else… but she didn't.

He lay on his back and stared at the ceiling. Every inch of him wanted to reach for her, to touch and comfort her through her pain and thoughts. He'd gone through what she was going through. The fleeting feeling of satisfaction, mixed with confusion and lingering anger, is still bottled up after decades of pain. Of wanting to get right back into the ring and hurt Odin all over again, yet knowing that doing so wouldn't make it feel better. Nothing made it feel better. Nothing erased the memories and the pain. Only time dulled the ache and the guilt. The guilt for not doing more. For not having saved more. For not having died herself. He knew it all. Had felt it all. And somehow, had made it out the other side of it. And she would too.

The covers rustled against her wings as she rolled over, eyes closed, her body facing his.

She was the most beautiful creature he'd ever laid eyes on. Strong and tall, delicate and willowy. A complex set of opposites that fascinated him.

Without a word, she scooted closer to him, eyes still closed. He waited, hoping, praying, and then his breath hitched as she nestled against him. A wave of overwhelming protectiveness washed over him, causing his heart to gallop with a mixture of longing and disbelief. The gentle weight of her head on his chest felt like a fragile miracle. She was touching him. Choosing him. He didn't know if it was the simple need to connect with another being or if she wanted to be closer to him specifically, but he didn't care. He would take whatever she would give him.

He adjusted his position, allowing their bodies to meld together. Every beat of his heart seemed to synchronize with hers as she settled in closer, her warmth seeping into his soul. He wrapped his arm around her back and down her soft wings. He traced his fingers through the downy feathers. She made a small sound he couldn't decipher as he studied her face. A purple bruise bloomed across her left cheek, but strangely, that was the only one. As if Odin had tried to spare her face from damage. Interesting considering Odin was known for his jabs and hooks. Yet the more he thought about it, the more he realized Odin hadn't used even a fraction of his strength through the entire fight. Not that many would have noticed, but it struck Loki how much Odin had pulled his punches with Val. Even before he'd given in to her need to release her rage on him.

He sighed, and for a split second, he pitied Odin. In so many ways, he'd taken on the brunt of everyone's anger at one point or another. Loki, Fenrir, Thor, Val, and so many others. Yet he never complained. Never made excuses. Simply allowed them their anger and then moved on.

Val's hand slid across Loki's chest and stopped short of wrapping around his torso in a hug. The soft sound of her snores brought a serenity to him. A silent acknowledgment of the precious trust she had placed in him. It was a victory he never dared to dream of, a moment of pure joy that reverberated through every fiber of his being. In the stillness of the night, he marveled at the privilege of being her guardian in slumber, cherishing the thought of being a source of comfort in a multiverse of uncertainties.

As he gazed upon her peaceful form, a resolve bloomed within him. He knew he couldn't be everything to her, but in that instant, holding her close was more than enough. And in the quiet embrace, Loki found solace in the simple connection. A connection never given to him in his hours of need. In his years of torture. In his eons of loneliness and pain.

He lowered his head, pressing his lips against the strands of her damp hair. Emotions surged and swirled within him, a tumultuous storm of unease. How could this be? He had battled giants, challenged gods, and vanquished enemies by the thousands. And yet… this one lone Valkyrie touched a place in him he didn't know he owned. He didn't know why she affected him the way she did, but… a haunting notion crept in. A notion so unbelievable it sent shivers down his spine. The possibility that she might be the one.

His one. His fated mate.

VAL AWOKE TO A SURGE OF PANIC CLAWING AT HER CHEST, ITS sharp edges slicing through the veil of sleep. Her eyes flickered open, scanning the unfamiliar surroundings that enveloped her in a shroud of disorientation. Where in the realms was she? A moment hung suspended, dangling on the edge of uncertainty, before the floodgates of memory burst wide open. Valhalla's Throne. The name echoed in her mind, a beacon amidst the haze of confusion.

Her body, a battlefield of sensations, throbbed with a dull ache. Tenderness lingered as she stretched before her fingers rubbed her neck and then traced the outline of a wing- a forgotten part of herself unearthed after years of concealment. How long had it been since she last soared freely? A longing surged within her. Yet, the harsh reality of Midgard meant her wings would not see the sky anytime soon. On Midgard, a woman with large white wings flying through the air wouldn't be wise. And down in Helheim... who knew who would spot her and trace her back to Elle.

A resigned sigh escaped her lips as she set her hand back where it had previously been. Her touch lingered, tracing patterns on a smooth surface, until realization dawned. Skin. Soft, hairless… muscles.

Loki.

Her eyes finally opened, and her gaze whipped up to his face. His features softened by the tranquility of sleep.

She swallowed against the tide of emotions threatening to engulf her. She'd fallen asleep on him. She'd never slept with anyone before. Sex, yes, but sleeping, no way. Yet she'd slept with Loki. Loki of all people. Sleeping beside him, a simple act laden with complexities she dared not unravel.

The Loki she'd heard about, and the Loki she'd experienced for herself, seemed like two different people. Maybe time really had changed him. After all, it had been hundreds of years since she'd last seen or heard about him. Hadn't she changed in the last hundred years?

She studied his face. His high cheekbones and slight stubble that crossed his chin. His long, dark hair loose around him, giving him a youthful appearance despite his age. The humans would call him a Metrosexual, at least that's what she thought. She'd read about it in a magazine. A man who dressed nicely, used skin and hair products, and took great care with his appearance. That was Loki to a T. She wanted nothing more than to touch his soft, shiny-looking hair.

What? Touching his hair? Had Odin hit her in the head? How stupid could she be? She'd seen women flirt before, especially the humans in the bar. But that was just plain silly schoolgirl crap.

Loki was a flirt, that was obvious, but she was not. Which was why it had surprised her so much that she'd flirted with Marek.

Marek. He'd been gone when her fight had ended. She wished that she'd at least been able to explain to him, but how could he ever understand her anger and pain toward Odin?

He couldn't. But Loki had. Loki had encouraged her to fight Odin. He'd not shied away from her pain and her rage, he'd... understood it. Understood her. No one had ever understood her before. Not that she'd given anyone the opportunity to try. She'd neither needed nor wanted it in the past. But with Loki... For some reason, she wanted him to understand her. To accept her. To help her believe she was lovable despite what she'd been through. What she'd endured.

"You are welcome to keep staring at me, but telling me how good-looking I am would really boost my ego," Loki said.

Val rolled her eyes. "As if your ego could get any bigger." She pushed against his chest to sit up, but he pulled her against him with the arm he had wrapped around her shoulders.

He opened his eyes. "Where are you going?"

"I should check on Elle."

"She's with Thor. She'll be fine."

"Will she?"

Loki chuckled. "Trust me, he's more smitten with Elle than he was when he lifted Mjölnir for the first time."

Val struggled to decide between the need to check on Elle and the strange comfort that it brought her, being wrapped in Loki's arms.

For a long moment, they stared at each other, and then quickly, Loki flipped her on her back and poised above her. He lingered for a moment before she reached up and touched a lock of his hair.

Yup. He definitely took better care of his hair than she did.

Loki bent in close to her, his lips lingering above hers.

No kissing. That was her rule. Always had been. Kissing was intimate, sensual. Neither thing she'd ever wanted to share with someone before. But... for some reason she couldn't fathom or escape, she wanted to feel his mouth on hers. To taste his lips.

"I... I've never kissed a man before," she admitted.

His eyebrows drew together. "Never?"

She shook her head. "Never let anyone. Never wanted to. It's always been my rule."

A dark desire crossed his eyes. "Is it still your rule?"

She touched his lips with her fingers. So soft. She wondered what kind of Chapstick he used.

He kissed her fingertip, and then she ran the pad of her finger between his lips and into his mouth. He reached out with his tongue and licked her finger before sliding the whole thing into his mouth. He bit down, sending shivers and waves of desire through her entire being. She pulled her finger from his mouth, and before he could protest, she pressed her lips to his. He didn't move for a second and then wrapped his arm around her further and pulled her against him. He parted his lips and slid his tongue down the seam of hers. He flicked his tongue against her mouth, coaxing her lips apart. When his tongue touched hers, her entire body melted in a rush of heat.

He kissed her soft, leading her, guiding her until she wanted nothing more than to feel him inside her.

She moved her fingers over the lean contours of his chest. Scars raised on his skin, and she touched them in turn, memorizing every single one.

He cupped her face in his hand and then reached down and lifted her leg over his hip. He ground into her core, making her mewl with need. She wanted him. Wanted him desperately. She moved her hand down to his belt buckle and undid it before sliding her hand down his pants.

Loki groaned and grabbed her hand through the fabric. "Slow down, love."

"Why? I want you. You want me."

"Because," he said. "I don't just want to have sex with you, I want to make love to you. The way you deserve to be loved."

Loved? Who said anything about love?

In that moment, desire burned within her with an intensity that eclipsed all else. The craving for him filled every corner of her being, drowning out the doubts and fears clawing at her. Love? A mere distraction, a fleeting notion compared to the urgent ache throbbing in her veins. But amidst the overwhelming passion, a sorrowful realization crept in, wrapping her in a shroud of isolation. Maybe, just maybe, amidst the flames of lust, there lingered a yearning for love. Perhaps she dared to hope for it, even in the arms of Loki-

"Signe," she blurted.

"What?"

"My name. My real name is Signe."

"Signe. Means one who is victorious. Quite fitting." He smiled.

The sound of her real name on his lips made her chest ache.

"I've never told anyone my true name before. Never heard anyone say it but my mother. Say it again," she whispered. She'd not heard her real name in so long that it almost sounded foreign.

Loki kissed her again. "Signe." He kissed across her cheek

to her ear. "Signe." He kissed down to her collarbone and licked across it. "Signe."

Tears formed in her eyes. Her name. Her true name. The one her mother gave her. She'd not told anyone. Not her sisters. Not Elle. Not even Elle's mother. But somehow hearing the name in Loki's deep voice was a balm to her soul that she'd not known she needed.

Loki kissed lower down over her breasts. Val pulled her arms from her torn shirt and tossed it to the floor. Loki admired her naked flesh and then bent down and suckled one of her breasts into his mouth. Val bucked against the feel of his lips as her skin pebbled and her nipples hardened. Her wings caressed her naked back in a soft cocoon.

Loki's hand cupped her other breast as he suckled the first one. Val ran her fingers through his hair, and he pressed his hips into hers, grinding against her.

Val moaned and pulled his mouth harder against her skin until she couldn't take any more. She slid her hand inside his underwear. Loki tensed and nipped at her breast, making her pant.

"I want you," she said.

Loki broke away from her breasts and kissed down her belly to her hips. He kissed over a bruise the size of a grapefruit, and she grimaced but didn't dare tell him to stop. He lowered the sweats and kissed her bare skin. She dug her hands into his hair as he lowered the pants more and more, kissing his way down her thighs to her toes. When he removed the fabric, he stood and shucked off his shoes and jeans.

Every inch of him was a giant mass of taut muscles. Not bulky and brawny, but lean like a panther. Agile and strong.

Loki crawled back onto the bed and proceeded to kiss from her toes up her thighs to the juncture between her legs. He buried his face in her and licked her from one end to the other. She gasped at his tongue rubbing over her most sensitive places. Val looked into Loki's eyes as he licked her throbbing center, a deep longing welling up inside her.

"Don't stop..." she panted.

Loki groaned and bit down softly on the sensitive skin of her inner thigh before answering with his tongue.

"Never..." He licked her harder and faster, and her body wound tight with need for release.

Val cried out, shaking violently as the first wave of pleasure wound tighter inside her.

"So good," she moaned, arching into his touch. Her wings spread wide, seeking purchase on the bed beneath her.

He pressed a finger deep inside her, and he stroked in perfect rhythm with his tongue, sending shivers of delight through her body. She couldn't believe how good it felt to finally let go, to trust someone enough to feel the raw intensity of emotion.

“Loki... I can't..." Her words caught in her throat as pleasure washed over her. She dug her nails into the sheets beneath them.

"Let go, Signe."

She didn't need to be asked twice. Her body shuddered, and she climaxed as his tongue continued to flick her nub and his fingers pressed in and out of her. Her body writhed and clenched as he worked her through her climax, and when she came down enough to breathe again, she let go of the headboard with a groan and panted limply against the mattress.

Loki continued taking his time with her as he kissed from her stomach to her mouth. She kissed him hungrily, wanting him inside her fully, but wanting to make sure he was taken care of as well.

"I've never... done that to a man before," she said. "But I'd like to return the favor if you'll be patient."

Loki kissed her again. "Not this time. This is about you, not me."

"Last time was about me. This time should be about both of us."

She'd never expected Loki to be a generous lover. There were so many different things that she thought she'd known about him that she'd been wrong about. It left her feeling both foolish and intrigued. What else didn't she know about him?

Loki hovered above her, his presence as intense as a summer thunderstorm on the verge of release. His lips traced a path down Val's neck. He took her breast into his mouth with a tenderness that sent shivers rippling through her body. Then, with a slow thrust of his hips, he was inside her, filling her.

Val moaned as she took in the length of him. It had been so long since she'd had a man inside her. But this wasn't just any man; it was Loki. A Norse god. And he absolutely was in every way.

Loki kissed her as he sucked in a breath and rocked inside her again and again. Moving with deliberate slowness, creating a rhythm almost musical, resonating within her like the low hum of ocean waves crashing on the sand.

"Harder," she gasped.

Loki chuckled. "No, love. Be patient." He kissed her again, letting his tongue swirl inside her mouth.

Her need for him to go harder dissipated as the coil of release built inside her again. Over and over, he rolled his hips into hers in an upward circular motion, causing him to rub against her sensitive nub and sending shockwaves through her. He kissed her, his hands roaming her body, squeezing and teasing her nipples until she once again spiraled close to the edge. With every gentle motion, she drew closer to an unknown place where sensation and emotion fused.

She wrapped her arms around Loki's back and dug her nails into his skin.

Loki growled, and his body tensed as he kissed her harder. Soon she pulled him into her and ground her hips against his, wanting him deeper. Her body heated, and sensations she'd never experienced before coursed through her. Need. Loss. Pleasure. Desire... Love.

Was that what he'd meant when he'd said he wanted to make love to her? Had he known doing what he did would open her up and make her vulnerable? Had that been his intention all along?

She didn't have a chance to think any more about it because she tumbled over the edge and climaxed again. As soon as she did, Loki pulled his lips from hers and stared into her eyes as his body tensed, and he climaxed as well. For a moment, his eyes turned icy, and his skin took on an ashy blue hue. Horns sprouted from the front of his skull and curled backward over his head. His face grew more angular as his eyes glowed with inner light. She blinked several times to see if she was imagining it, but the image didn't leave. A *Jötunn.* He really was a *Jötunn.*

He leaned in and kissed her hard. His lips crushed hers against his, his breathing labored. When he broke the kiss, he appeared as he always did. No horns, no ashen skin, no glowing icy eyes. Just his handsome, tanned face and dark, wavy hair. She'd imagined it… or had she? Was his whole image a facade?

He kissed her forehead before rolling over on his side and pulling her into him. She wrapped her arms around him and clung to him for several seconds as she replayed the image in her head.

"Did I hurt you?" he asked.

"Why would you think that?"

"The expression on your face. It was... pained almost." Fear tinged his voice, or possibly anxiety.

She sat up and searched his face. Did he not realize what had happened when he climaxed?

"I saw you," she said.

His eyebrows drew together. "And I saw you."

She shook her head. "No. I mean... I saw you. The real you. Why do you hide who you are?"

His gaze flickered, and terror struck his features for a moment before he swallowed. "Why do you hide your wings? Or your feelings? Or your name?"

She didn't need to answer. They both knew why.

"Show me," she whispered.

Loki looked at her for a long time without speaking, as if silently pleading with her not to ask it of him.

“I want to see you,” she urged. In the last hours, he'd seen her at some of her worst, and he'd learned her real name. Something was changing between them, and she needed him to know he was as safe with her as she was with him.

The air around him shimmered, and the facade fell away. There on the bed lay the real Loki. Longer limbed and a full head taller than before. His skin was a pale, dusty blue, his eyes like sky-blue diamonds, and large, smooth black horns protruded from his forehead, curving upward.

He waited, not breathing, not moving.

She reached out and touched his cheek, and then moved her hand up to his horns. They were warm and smooth as glass. She continued to run her fingers all the way to the sharp points at the end and then traced her hand through his hair and down to his hard chest. His heartbeat thumped against her palm where she rested it.

"Will you leave now?" he asked. "Ashamed and horrified for having lain with a monster?"

Val smiled. "I've been bedded by monsters before, and I have news for you, Loki, god of mischief and *Jötunn*, you are no monster."

Loki's eyes clouded with emotion. He reached out and pulled her mouth to his before kissing her and then setting his forehead against hers. "You are like no woman I have ever met."

"And you are like no man I have ever met."

Loki looked at her seriously. "Maybe that is because we were only meant for each other, Signe."

Her chest squeezed, and she fought to find words, but had none. Could it be true? Could Loki be the one she'd been waiting for?

CHAPTER NINE

Loki knew his words sounded stupid, sappy, and pathetic, but somehow, she brought out a soft side of him. Something about Val- Signe had awoken in him a need and a tenderness that he'd never possessed before. Plus, she'd seen him, the true him, and she'd not run away. He'd shown his true self only once to his former wife. It had scared her so badly that for months she'd not even been able to look at him, until he finally erased the memory from her mind. But Val had not only not run from him, but she'd also asked to see his true form again, and even touched him.

His whole life, he'd learned early to hide that part of his heritage for the prejudice that came with it. But now... now he wondered if with her help he might become comfortable enough to walk around in his own skin. It was funny, in Helheim, he was less likely to be looked at twice in his true form, but he'd gotten so used to looking like everyone else to fit in that he'd never tried it.

"What time is it?" she asked.

Loki looked at his watch. "It's close to five a.m."

She nodded. "I really should go. Though you believe Elle is in no danger with Thor around, I would feel better if I saw for myself."

"If that is what you wish." What he really wanted was to spend the entire day in bed with her in his arms, but she wouldn't feel at ease again until she knew Elle was safe. Loki wondered what it would be like to have someone care for and worry about him like that.

"I need my clothes."

He nodded. "They should be in a basket outside the door. But before you put them on, let me check your wings again."

"They feel better."

"I would feel better if I saw for myself."

A smile played on her lips as he used her own words against her. She turned around and spread her wings as wide as she was able. He looked them over, and the quills he had pulled from them had already begun to grow new feathers. The ones he had cut also looked healthier and had begun to fill in again. He touched her wing joint and bent her wing.

"The joints are tight from not being used and being folded away too long. If you'd waited much longer, they may have atrophied, and you would never use them again."

"Then I guess it's a good thing I didn't wait."

Loki sighed. "You need to take better care of yourself."

"Do I now?" She looked at him over her shoulder as she folded her wings away.

He kissed her bare shoulder. "Or I could do it for you."

She smiled, and then her smile fell. "I should go." She

grabbed the ripped sweatshirt from the floor and pulled it on before walking to the door and opening it. She picked up the basket with her clothes.

Loki watched her dress, sad that her beautiful body was hidden beneath the clothes. Even her T-shirt had been mended from where it had been shredded on the back by her wings. He wondered what kind of magic they used to fix it.

Then, as Val pulled on her boots, he stood and snapped his fingers. His clothes appeared once more.

"You know that's a neat trick," she said. "Maybe next time you can help me dress faster as well."

Loki smiled. "I would be more than happy to get you undressed fast." He snapped his fingers, and her clothing disappeared.

She looked down and nodded. "Cute. I mean, I don't mind walking through Helheim naked, but you might not want me to."

"Damn right." Loki snapped his fingers, and her clothing reappeared. He cupped her face. "I never want any other being to see you naked again besides me."

Conflict clouded her eyes.

Too much. He'd said too much.

He kissed her forehead. "But those things can wait. For now, let's go see if Elle is safe."

She nodded. "Sounds like a plan."

As Val and Loki exited Valhalla's Throne, the air was cool but not uncomfortable to her exposed skin. So many different feelings and thoughts rumbled through her that she couldn't settle on anything in particular. So instead, she settled on returning to her apartment. Once she'd done that, then she'd try to sort through everything that had happened in the past twelve hours.

"Are you ever going to talk to me again?" asked Loki.

She glanced over at him and snorted. "I think that's supposed to be my line."

He smiled. "For some reason, I can't see you asking a guy that."

"You'd be correct." Or would he? She could strangely see herself at least thinking it with him.

They walked another block in silence.

"So, is that a no?" he asked. "You one of those love 'em and leave 'em types?"

Her eyebrows scrunched together. "Why wouldn't I talk to you again? I mean, I didn't tell you my real name only to ignore you using it for the rest of existence. Because I'm pretty sure when you are sufficiently annoyed with me, you will use it."

He looked at her and then reached for her hand.

"Okay, that's too much." She pulled away. "I'm not twelve."

Loki barked out a laugh. "Maybe I am."

She snorted. "Twelve hundred more, like."

Val smiled as the scent of brimstone and blood hit her nostrils. She stopped and scanned the area.

"What's wrong?"

The hairs stood up on her arms. “We're being watched.”

She turned in a circle, scanning for something out of place. Loki stood at her back, and they turned in unison.

“You run, I'll handle this.”

Val snorted. “Seriously? I'm not a damsel in distress.”

Footsteps padded out of the shadows across the street.

"At least stay behind me," said Loki.

She raised an eyebrow at him. "You're joking, right? I have my weapons. Maybe you should stay behind me."

"Not on your life."

She pulled her sword from her back and extended it to its full length.

"Who are you?" Loki called. "What do you want?"

Six beings stopped halfway across the street. A mismatched crew of otherworldly beings. Among them, four seemed like males; one was a female, and another was impossible to pin down. Each demon stood out with its own unique flair. Skins that ranged from the deepest midnight blue to burning copper, heights varying from shorter than Elle to taller than Loki. Some had leathery wings tucked tight against their backs, two had an extra set of limbs, and all had horns spiraling in different directions out of their mouths or skulls.

Despite their incredible diversity, they all shared one glaring issue: they didn't belong in Helheim.

Demons stuck to the other realms of the Underworld. Helheim belonged to Hel. Demons from other realms needed permission to visit. It was the same with every realm of the Underworld. A way that Lucifer kept control of who went where and who spoke to whom. The last thing he needed was realms joining together to try to overthrow him.

"We want the woman," the male in front called.

"Sorry, she's taken," Loki replied.

She glared at him, and he winked back at her.

“Now isn’t the time to irritate me,” she said.

"Rumor has it there is a sizable bounty on her head, as well as a girl she travels with. Give them to us, and we'll share them with you," said a female.

Loki looked at them like they'd each grown a dozen heads. "Do you have any idea who I am?"

"Nope. And we don't care. All we want is the women. Give them to us, and we'll let you live."

"Now, hold on," said Val. "What the hel makes you think he has the right to give you anything? I belong to no one. If I want to go with him, I will. If I want to go with you, I will. If I want to sever your heads from your ever pathetic bodies, I will. No one owns me."

"Sever their heads?" asked Loki. "How boring. I could think of a thousand different ways to kill them that would be much more fun."

Val sighed. "I'm not looking for fun. I'm tired. I want to finish this and go to bed."

"Ooooohhhh am I invited this time?" He wiggled his eyebrows at her.

Val rolled her eyes.

"What is wrong with you two?" asked the tallest male in front. "Don't you realize there are six of us and only two of you? She can come now, and we'll let you both live. Or you can resist, and we'll kill you both. Nowhere in the bounty does it say she needs to be alive."

Loki and Val looked at each other.

"They don't know who I am," said Loki. "I don't know whether I should be astonished or insulted."

"I'd say insulted. But then they don't know me either, so..."

"But you aren't a god."

"Former god, if you want to be technical. Now you're just a lawyer."

Loki's jaw dropped. "That hurt, love. That hurt."

"Enough! Get the woman. Kill the man," the leader yelled.

The group attacked. Two with wings took to the air and rose above them. Two more ran across the street on all fours. Only the leader and the female hung back for a moment.

"Guess it's time to exercise those wings again," said Loki as he produced two icy blue glowing curved blades from thin air.

Val extended her wings and rose into the air. The demons flew straight for her, but she pulled in her wings and spiraled between them. She slashed out with her sword, catching one of their wings and slicing it clean off. The demon spiraled out of control and hurdled downward, where he crashed into the cobblestone and bounced into a building. The second demon spun around and headed back toward her. A stream of acid flew her direction, and she barely missed being hit by it as she lifted higher. Down below, Loki fought with the demons who had scampered across the road. She needed to stop screwing around and help him.

The demon flew at her again, talons out. Val threw her sword, and it planted in the demon's chest. He dropped to the ground, missing Loki.

"Hey. Careful up there. We're on the same side."

"It's not my fault these guys are so weak they can't even take one hit," she replied.

Val dove to the ground and pulled her knives from her belt. She spun and slashed the throat of one of the demons before plunging her other knife deep into its neck, taking the thing's head clean off.

“Looks like you got your wish,” Loki teased.

She growled. "Stop playing around. I told you I am tired."

Loki threw his blade, and it stuck in the side of one of the demon's neck. He leaped onto the demon and pulled the blade from its neck before stabbing it through the chest.

“Sorry, love. I didn’t get to fight last night as you did. I wanted a bit of a challenge.”

“I’ll give you a challenge if you don’t stop messing around.” She rushed and retrieved her sword before strapping it to her back again.

The last of the demons stopped and scanned the already spreading carnage. It backed up a pace and looked at the male leader, who hadn't moved from his spot in the road.

"Well," said Val. "Are you going to come get me, or are we going to keep dicking around looking at each other?"

The male looked at the female and then at the demon who had backed up to his side.

"Okay then, I guess I'll come to you." Val flew at them, and the three demons scattered.

The female went right, and the male went left. The stupid one ran straight at her. But before she stabbed it, Loki appeared in front of her and cut off the demon's head.

"I'm anxious for your challenge." Loki winked at her before taking off toward the male.

Val flew down the street after the female. She caught up with her and kicked the female in the back. The demon tumbled to the ground and rolled over several times. Val landed on top of her and dropped on the demon's chest. The female gasped but couldn't get up. Val knelt on her throat and held her knife up.

"Where did you hear about me?" she demanded.

The demon shook her head. "I... didn't. Canax did."

See.. There was that stupid ending in 'ax' name again. "Who told him?"

The woman shook her head again. "I don't know. I swear."

"Then who put the bounty on me?" Val pressed harder against the woman's neck.

"Someone outside of Helheim in a different part of the Underworld. I don't know who. Canax never told me. He just said you were worth a lot of money, and if we brought you and the girl in, we could get enough to move up to a better realm."

"Did they say who the girl was?"

She shook her head. "They said you would lead us to her."

Like hel she would. "How long have you been following me?"

"Tonight. You were spotted going into Valhalla's Throne."

"Anything else?" Val asked.

"No. I swear."

Val nodded. "I believe you." She slit the demon's throat. "But I can't let you tell anyone else. Sorry."

The demon's eyes widened as she choked on her own blood, and then her mouth stopped moving. Val stabbed her in the heart for good measure and stood.

She turned and rushed back down the alley to find Loki standing over the body of the decapitated leader of the group.

Damn. She'd been hoping to find out who told them about a bounty. But then again, she had told Loki she wanted to cut all their heads off. At least he'd listened to her for once.

Val flew back down the road. Loki flipped his blades in the air, and they disappeared.

"You all right?" Loki asked, looking over her.

She nodded. "You?"

"Never better. How are your wings?" He turned her around and pulled out her wings.

“Oh my gosh, you are as bad as a wet nurse.” She pulled away from him and wiped black blood on her pants before putting her knives away. Her heart pounded with adrenaline, and she realized how good it felt to get in the air, even if it was for only a few minutes.

"We should go topside," said Loki.

"Oh, now you want me topside?"

"Until I can figure out who is talking down here about a bounty, yes. You need to stay in Midgard. Especially if it’s bringing in demons from other realms."

Val nodded. "Agreed."

"Wait." Loki put his hand on her arm.

"What?"

"Friday."

"Friday?" she asked.

"Odin invited us to dinner." He started walking down the street.

"So?"

Loki shook his head. "You don't get it. When there is a family dinner, you don't say no. You go."

She shrugged. "Okay, you go. I'm not family."

"But he invited you."

"Still doesn't make me family, so I don't have to go."

They continued down the street and turned the corner.

"If he invited you, you can guarantee that he invited Elle as well."

"That's a hel of a big fat no. There is no way she's coming down here. Not after what just happened. I don't ever want her down here again."

"That might be a bit hard, considering she's pretty much dating Thor now, and he lives down here."

"Look." She stopped and blew out a breath. She didn't want to talk about his family. "I'm tired, and I need at least some sleep before work in a few hours. Can we… not talk about this?"

Loki shrugged. "Sure. But that's not going to change the situation. So, I guess I'll have to work fast to figure out who is in contact with Surtr."

She slowed her pace. "How do you know it's Surtr?"

"Are there other people who want you dead or alive I should know about? I mean, I'm all up to protect you, but it would be nice to know how many murderous maniacs I need to be on the lookout for."

"Haha. You are so funny."

"And good-looking, right? I'm funny and good-looking."

She rolled her eyes. "Yeah, sure."

"What about good in bed. I'm really good in bed, aren't I? Like great. Excellent, in fact."

"Enough with the compliments for one night. Your head is big enough already."

"Which head? My cranium or my-"

Val turned, grabbed Loki by the shirt, and pressed her lips to his. "Shut up," she whispered. "If you ever want to see me naked again. You will shut up."

Loki nodded. "Noted." He grabbed her hand and laced his fingers in hers. "But if I can't talk to you, then I get to hold your hand at least."

She opened her mouth, but he kissed her again. "Humor me."

She blew out a breath. She had to admit that the feel of his fingers laced with hers did give her a sense of calm. She wanted to fight him, but in the end, she allowed the contact, and they continued to the bar.

They walked up the stairs to her apartment and stopped by Elle's door. She pulled her hand from Loki's and raised it to knock, but stopped when the toilet flushed inside.

"See, she's fine," said Loki. "No harm. No kidnappers. Nothing."

Val sighed inwardly. Elle was safe. Now she needed to make sure Elle stayed that way.

Loki pulled her down the hallway to her own apartment and stopped at the door. "So, are you going to let me in?"

She wanted to. Hel knew she wanted to. But she shouldn't. She should go inside- alone- and try to figure things out.

"I'm really tired," she lied.

Loki nodded and shoved his hands into his pockets. "I get it."

She turned to him. "Get what?"

"I'll go. But give some thought to coming on Friday. Especially since I can't promise Odin won't come up here to get you if you don't show."

"See, it's that aggressive, 'do what I say or else', bullshit that made me hate him in the first place."

"Join the club."

They stared at each other in awkward silence for a minute, and then Loki nodded. "Well... It was fun fighting by your side."

"More fun than having me hide behind you?"

He thought for a moment. "Actually, yes. I can't remember the last time I had a real fight, nor can I remember the last time I had someone decent to fight alongside."

"You're not so bad yourself. I'd do it again if I had to."

"Had to? Really? If you had to." He clutched his chest in mock offense and stepped forward, leaning close. "I would do anything you asked me to, even saving your life, just to be near you."

She leaned in closer until their lips almost touched. "You think you saved my life? That's cute."

He grinned. "You know… I can name a dozen things off the top of my head I'd enjoy you doing with that wicked tongue besides always putting me in my place."

His words punched her in the gut, but she couldn't help the smile that spread across her lips. "You and I both know it's my wicked tongue that caught your attention in the first place."

"Actually, it was your eyes that caught me first. But it's your tongue that keeps me coming back for more. That and… other things."

Her smile widened. "What other things?"

He chuckled and took a step back. "Goodnight, Signe."

His use of her name sent a thrill rushing through her.

He gave her a flourishing bow and then turned to leave.

"Loki?"

He stopped. "Yes?"

She walked to him and shoved her hands in his back pockets. "I think I'll talk to you again."

He smiled. "Today?"

She laughed. "Are you being pushy or just clingy?"

"How about we say I'm persistent. When I find something I want, I go for it and don't let anything stand in my way." Loki cupped her face and pulled her lips to his. "And I want you, Signe. Every part of you."

Her heart shuddered when his lips touched hers. She squeezed his butt and pulled his hips into hers. He backed her into the wall and pressed against her. His kisses heated, and his hands brushed over her breasts before he rolled his thumbs over her nipples. Val couldn't hold back the moan that escaped her throat. Her core spasmed. She wanted him again.

"Loki," she panted.

"Signe." He nipped at her ear.

"I... I think we should continue this inside my apartment."

He kissed her hard, and she plunged her tongue into his mouth, claiming it. He pulled away suddenly, leaving her panting.

"Not now," he said. "Now, you need some sleep."

She shook her head, trying to comprehend his words through the haze of desire. "Are you serious?"

He nodded and then kissed the tip of her nose. "I want you to think about me today. While you're sleeping. While you're showering. While you're working. I want you to think about me good and hard, and then when you see me again, I'll let you know those dozen things I'll let you do to me with your tongue. And maybe a few I'll do to you with mine." He kissed her cheek and then headed back toward the stairs.

Val's mouth fell open. He was serious. He was going to leave her hot and bothered and needing release.

Touché, Loki. Touché.

CHAPTER TEN

Despite a night with little sleep, Val felt surprisingly invigorated. Satisfied? Maybe even on the verge of happy? No, she couldn't quite claim that yet.

She unfurled her wings, letting them catch the warm morning light that streamed through the window. The warmth danced across the feathers. They looked better today. She ran her fingers over one that Loki cut, remembering how tenderly he'd cared for them and her after the fight. She'd never expected that of him, gentleness, selflessness, caring. The memory sent an unexpected flutter through her chest, one she tried to suppress. Dangerous territory, letting herself feel anything for the Trickster. Yet she couldn't deny something had shifted between them last night. Something she wasn't ready to name.

Name… her name… she'd told him her name. She had no idea why she'd done it, only that she'd suddenly wanted him to know her real name. To say her real name. To hear him call her by it… and he had.

And what about him? He'd shown her his true form. Not the one he used as a mask to blend in, but the real him. Beautiful and tall, muscular with those alluring horns.

Never once in Muspelheim had she ever been attracted to one of the fire giants. But Loki with his light blue skin and icy eyes… she had no idea why she found them even more desirable as his true self, but she did.

Her mind turned to how he'd left her hours before, wanting more… Well, if he thought that game would work on her, he was mistaken. She wouldn't be a toy.

She tucked her wings back into place, and they disappeared into her skin. She stretched and groaned, grabbing her ribs where they ached from her fight with Odin. Her gaze drifted outwards again, yearning for the open sky. Work called first, and Elle's well-being was paramount. Maybe she could return to Helheim and fly- Nope. She needed to stay on Midgard until Loki figured out who had talked to the demons and how they'd gotten into Helheim.

When Val walked down the stairs, Marek already sat at the bar. Her stomach dropped. It would be easier if he didn't come in anymore, but she couldn't throw him out because he hadn't been able to handle what she held inside. He had as much right to drink at a bar as she did to work in one.

She walked over. The other bartender nodded as Val washed her hands and scanned to see what needed refilling. She felt Marek's eyes on her back, but wasn't ready to face him. What did she say?

Oh, hey. Sorry you saw me go wackadoo on Odin last

night. I'm really not that much of a freak, but you know, he ripped me from my mom when I was little and forced me to fight in his army until I was the only one left, and then I was kidnapped by a sadist. So...

Yeah, that would go over well.

For several minutes, Val did everything possible to ignore Marek, but when he called for a drink, she had no choice but to pay attention to him.

"Hi," he said.

Val nodded. "Marek. What can I get you?"

"Beer is fine."

She picked up his empty glass and turned to go, but he touched her hand.

"I'm sorry for leaving last night."

She shrugged. "No biggie."

His eyes held sadness and shame. "I... I wasn't prepared to see you... like that."

"You mean fight? That surprises me, with you being a wolf and all. I would assume you'd seen people fight a million times."

"I have, but not like that. You were... I don't know. Obsessed?"

Val blew out a breath. "I'm not for everyone. I carry more baggage than a cargo plane. Even so, I'm sorry you had to see me like that, but I'm glad you did now rather than after we started something. I'm broken inside, and even I can't handle it a lot of times. So, no hard feelings."

He looked down at the bar and nodded. "You're probably right."

Val wanted to say something to comfort him and make

him feel better, but what would do that? And why should she have to comfort him? He saw who she was, what she was, and if he couldn't handle that, that wasn't her problem. Still, he'd been nothing but a gentleman to her.

She held out her hand. "Friends?"

He looked up at her and smiled. "Friends."

He chuckled.

"What?"

"I was just thinking that I'm usually the one people go to when they need help with someone or something. I've never had anyone I could go to. But seeing you in action last night made me think that if I ever were in trouble, I'd come to you for help."

Val laughed. "Anytime."

Marek studied her.

She rolled her eyes. "What now?"

"You seem... happier today. More relaxed."

Val's cheeks heated despite her protests.

Marek nodded. "I'm glad you've found someone who makes you smile. Wish it could have been me, but if not, at least it's a Norse god. He'd better take care of you. Or Norse god or not, he will have to deal with me."

She smiled. She hadn't felt like anyone had her back since she'd been with her sisters.

"Thanks."

Take care of her? Did she want Loki to take care of her? She liked being self-reliant. But then again, it would be nice to have someone looking out for her for a change. She had no idea what that would feel like, and if she could even give up control long enough to let him.

"I gotta go," said Marek. "I just stopped by to apologize."

"What about your beer?"

He shook his head. "I gotta get back to work. I'll see ya around Valkyrie."

"You know, there is a bottom side to this bar. Down… below. You should get a drink there sometime. Talk to Lady Frigg, she's the owner, and ask her about her monthly masquerade. Maybe you'll meet someone."

Marek stared at her for a moment. "I might just do that. Thanks."

She watched him go. "Marek," she called. "What do you do for work?"

Marek smiled. "I'm a veterinarian."

Could he be sweeter? Kind. Gentle. And cares for animals? Why couldn't she fall for a guy like that instead of the god of mischief? The answer was simple- nice, sweet, guys could never handle her. She would chew them up and leave them in a puddle. What she really needed was a man like Loki, whether she wanted him or not. Only a man like Loki, sharp, annoying, endearing, and as broken as she was, would do. A man who kept her on her feet but satisfied her while on her back.

Her cheeks heated again as Marek waved and walked out the door.

What the hell did she mean she was falling for Loki? She hadn't fallen for Loki. She'd have fun with Loki. Used Loki for release, but- She stopped. Who was she kidding? She'd told Loki things she'd not told another person. That wasn't something you did with someone you used for great sex. Her heart thundered. Loki. She was falling for Loki... She couldn't let that happen. She couldn't. Falling in love with Loki was bound to lead her to the one thing she'd avoided for a thousand years. A broken heart.

"Hi, Val." Elle approached the bar.

"Elle." Val poured two drinks and put them on a tray.

"How... how are you?"

Val looked up. Elle was trying. It was written all over Elle's face that she didn't want Val to be mad at her. She never could handle people being angry with her. It was one of the things she'd been working on with Elle before they'd left. She'd tried so hard to please everyone, and yet there was no way she was going to be able to do that.

"I'm great. How are you?"

Elle blinked several times. "Great? I've never heard you say that word before."

Val shrugged. "I've never felt great before."

"What makes you feel so great? Did something good happen? Did you meet someone? The werewolf guy who was just here. Is it him?" Elle beamed from ear to ear.

"No. Marek and I are friends. I..." She what? She got laid several times for the first time in a hundred years, and she felt more relaxed than she had in forever. She couldn't say that. "I went to Odin's fight club last night and let off some steam. And then I stretched my wings for a bit."

"You got in a fight? Were you hurt?" Elle's eyes filled with concern.

"I won." Though that was only because Odin let her.

"Oh. Well, I'm glad then."

Val pushed the tray of drinks to Elle. "You should take these to your table before they get upset."

Elle nodded and took the tray.

Val got the feeling that Elle wanted her to ask how it had gone with Thor, but she couldn't. To be honest, she didn't want to know. Didn't want to know it had gone well and that Elle would be seeing more of Thor.

Loki had told her Thor truly cared for Elle, so in the end, she guessed it really wasn't her business. At least Elle had made that clear with the way she'd acted a couple of days prior. And as much as it bothered Val that Elle had talked to her that way and stuck up for Thor, it had also made Val proud. She'd never seen nor heard Elle be that assertive before.

Val looked at the clock. She'd only been at work thirty minutes, and already she wanted to leave. She wanted nothing more than to go back up to her apartment and take a nap. Something she'd not done, ever as far as she could remember. Though she wouldn't mind sharing a nap with Loki- even though they wouldn't get much sleep. Again.

Loki walked into the topside of the Raven Weaver uneasily. He'd found out who had been in contact with Surtr, but he wasn't going to be as easy to deal with as Loki had hoped. And he'd been forced into making a deal with the demon that Val was going to kill him for.

He strode to the bar and sat right in front of her, not bothering to ask for a drink or hide his true intention. This wasn't the time to play around. Val would want to be told straight up and right away. She finished serving several beers and then looked at him and smiled. He wasn't sure he'd really seen her smile at him before. She'd laughed at him, but smiled, genuinely smiled, that was something new. Which made what he was about to tell her all the more difficult.

She walked to him. "Did you find out anything?"

"Do you have a few minutes for a break?"

Her eyes narrowed, and then she nodded. "Sure."

"Can we go up to your place?" he asked.

"I don't think we have that much time," she said.

"Not for sex. I just think we should talk in private."

Her expression darkened. "All right." She turned to the other bartender. "I'm taking my fifteen."

The other bartender waved.

Val scanned the bar and then looked at him again. Loki stood and followed Val up the stairs. They'd barely gotten inside her apartment when she rounded on him.

"What's wrong?" She crossed her arms over her chest.

Loki closed the door and looked around her sparse apartment. The place smelled of sweet coffee and the faint cleaning product Frigg used on her floors. The walls were the color of old bone, the kind of off-white that came standard in every furnished unit. Efficient and no-frills, it contained all the items Frigg usually furnished, nothing more. No knick-knacks. No personal items. Nothing to signify anyone had even moved in.

“Well?” she pressed.

"I found out who is looking to cash you and Elle in to Surtr." He walked to the small wooden table and sat.

"What's the problem? Tell me who he is and where to find him, and I'll take care of it."

Loki unbuttoned his suit coat and crossed his legs. "That's the problem. I can't tell you."

"Why not?" she demanded.

"Because he is a client of mine and there are laws I have to follow."

"Human laws."

"Yes, but still laws. I am expected to follow the same rules down in the Underworld as I do up here. My clients rely on my discretion. If I break that oath, I'll lose my clients."

She shrugged. "So what? You don't need to work. You must have plenty of money. And I'm sure the humans pay better."

"It's not the money, love. It's the boredom. I have to do something to fill my eternity. You have bartending, I have my law practice. That right was bestowed on me by Lucifer himself. If I break it, I'll have more problems than just losing clients. I'll probably be kicked out of the Underworld, or locked up and tortured, or both. And I've had enough torture for one eternity."

"Well, if you aren't going to tell me, why did you call me all the way up here?" She shook her head and stomped toward the door.

Loki appeared in front of her, blocking her way. "I can't tell you who he is, but I can tell you where he will be."

She chewed the inside of her cheek. "Okay."

"Trust me, I want nothing more than to rip him apart myself, but I'm not allowed. However, I made him a deal."

"What kind of deal?"

The kind she wasn't going to like. "He's agreed to meet you tonight at Valhalla's Throne. He said if you can beat him in the cage, he'll stop looking for you and tell Surtr you aren't in the Underworld."

"And if I lose?"

"Then he gets to take you and Elle to Surtr."

"What? Hel no. Why would I agree to that?"

"You don't have to. If you don't show, he'll leave and keep hunting you. If you don't want to chance it, then keep hiding up here and wait him out. But if you do beat him, you'll never have to look over your shoulder again."

Val chewed her lip and stared at him. "Do you think I can beat him?"

"Absolutely." He threw her his best reassuring smile.

She cocked an eyebrow at him. "The truth."

His smile faltered. "I do. It won't be easy, but since he can't use any of his magical abilities, I think you can. Though I can't say what state you will be in when you are done."

She thought for a moment. "Will you take care of me when I'm injured?"

Loki's erection jumped to life. Hel yeah, he would take care of her. "Anything you need, love."

A slight smile played over her lips. "You better not promise something you aren't willing to or can't do."

"Is this a test?"

"If you want it to be."

Desire coursed through Loki. He liked nothing more than a challenge. And damn if she wasn't the best challenge he'd ever faced.

Loki took a step toward her and laced his fingers in the hair at the base of her neck.

"You might be the death of me, woman."

She pulled his hips against hers. "I sure hope not. What fun would you be if I could kill you so easy? I'd feel betrayed that so many had lied about your stamina."

Loki groaned at the feel of her svelte body pressed against his. He leaned in and kissed her neck. "Last night didn't convince you of my stamina?"

She chuckled. "You call that stamina? Now I do feel betrayed. I'm now wondering if the reason you left me unfulfilled by my door this morning is because that's all you had."

Loki growled and kissed her hard. So that's how she was going to play it. She wanted to see stamina; he would show her. He'd simply been trying to be gentle with her. But if that's not what she wanted… He'd show her exactly how much he wanted her. He'd already had her several times, but it still wasn't enough. He doubted he could make love to her a thousand times and tire of her.

She pressed him back against the door and kissed him harder. Her passion heated him all the more. Her hands roamed his body and grabbed his rear as she continued kissing him with gusto. She bit his bottom lip, and Loki pulled away as his desire spiked.

"I thought you said you didn't have time," he teased.

She smiled and stripped off her shirt to reveal the curves of her breasts, nipples already begging for his mouth. "I lied."

There was no going slow. No time to warm her up or make sure she had all her needs met. The air between them crackled like a live wire, raw and electric with need. She clawed at her pants, like they had offended her.

He barely had time to blink before she was naked, her skin flushed. The scent of her arousal hit him like a punch to the gut, thick and musky, making him throb painfully against his zipper. She'd stripped off her clothes and stood naked before he got his pants off.

"Snap them off," she commanded.

He didn't want to show off, but hel if she wanted him naked that bad, he wouldn't complain. With a snap, his clothes disappeared.

She stalked to him and cupped his length. "Now, take off your glamour."

He froze. He'd never stood naked in front of anyone without his glamour before. Doing so felt like being more than naked. It was like tearing down the wall he used to protect himself from every other being.

"Don't tell me you're suddenly shy."

"No, it's not that, it's just…" How did he explain?

"I want to see you. To feel you. The real you."

Her eyes traveled over his face, searching, probing.

With a knot in his gut, he let the magic fall off his skin. Her gaze softened, and she touched his face.

"I like the real you."

His heart squeezed so hard he fought the tears threatening to spill from his eyes. Loki grabbed her and picked her up, pinning her to the wall.

She laughed and looked down. "I feel closer to the ceiling than the floor now. How tall are you?"

"I'm not sure. Maybe seven feet."

She reached up and stroked his horns, sending sensations trickling over his scalp and down his neck that he'd never experienced, heightening his pleasure.

He couldn't hold back any longer, so he entered her hard

and fast.

She shuddered and grabbed his horns tighter. "You're so much bigger everywhere," she moaned, pressing her lips to his.

He thrust into her again, her body smaller, tighter, but not weaker. She took his entire length and mewled, wanting more of him. He'd never been so turned on by a woman in his life.

Something inside him broke open as she accepted him, took him in fully, and still wanted more.

She moved her hips back and forth, grinding onto him.

"Faster," she whispered. "My break is almost over."

Loki grabbed her by the neck as he thrust into her again. She moaned, and her head fell back as he leaned in and licked her throat.

"Loki," she moaned.

The sound of his name almost sent him over the edge.

"Loki," she panted again.

"Signe." He bit her shoulder, and she shuddered. "Signe... I love you." The words tumbled from his lips.

Had he just said that? Had he really told her he loved her? Shit. Why had he said that? What had made him confess that? He had no idea, but he also knew that it was the truth. As much as he never thought it would happen, there it was. She'd taken his walls and bulldozed them, shattered them, ground them to dust, and stood on the remains. And all that remained was his truth. His raw, real truth. He loved her.

She pulled his face to hers and kissed him before searching his eyes. "Tell me again," she whispered.

His chest squeezed. "I love you, Signe. I know it doesn't make sense, but I do."

She didn't speak for a minute, and he thought she might

push him away; instead, she pulled his mouth to hers and kissed him before setting her head against his. "Are you saying that because I'm a good lay?"

"I've never told a woman I loved her before. Ever. No matter how good they were in bed," he confessed. "Not when they asked me to. Not when I knew it was what they wanted to hear."

"Do you think that's what I want to hear?"

He shook his head. "Quite the opposite. I'm positive that's the last thing you want to hear, love."

She kissed him again. "Then I accept your words as truth. And now I want you even more."

She pushed her hips into his, and Loki turned with her and walked to the bed and dropped onto it. She flipped him onto his back and straddled him. Loki dug his fingers into her hips as she ground against him, sending waves of pleasure up the back of his legs and making his thighs burn.

She moaned and hummed as her friction increased and she rode him harder and faster. Her wings burst from her back and fanned out beautifully in the sunlight.

Loki held out from the climax that wound tight inside him. She was so beautiful. So perfect. He wanted every piece of her. And he wanted to see it. Wanted to see her climax. Wanted to watch her fall over that edge between pain and ecstasy.

It didn't take long. Her nails dug into his chest, and then she sucked in a sharp breath. He tried to rock her through her climax, but the sight of her beautiful, strong body, mixed with her calling his name, was so blissfully erotic he couldn't hold back.

His body exploded as he came. Every muscle in his body

tightened, and he no longer controlled his muscles. His eyes closed as the euphoria washed over him, but she hooked a finger in his mouth, and he opened his eyes again to find her watching him as she called his name again.

Finally, they both finished, she fell onto his chest, where her heartbeat through his own ribcage. He rubbed her back, touching where her skin met her wings. Her wings twitched and folded down flush against her skin. Their hearts beat in unison, and she ran her fingers down his arm and laced her fingers in his much larger ones before kissing his chest.

She looked up at him. "You are much more handsome in your true form. But I want you to save it only for me. For now, at least. I don't want to share this part of you with anyone. And whenever we make love, I want you to be in your natural form."

"Because I'm so much bigger?"

She bit his chest, and he laughed.

"No," she finally said. "Because I want us to be able to be completely open with each other. If we're going to do this, I don't want you to hide anything from me, and I need to know that I can fully be myself with you as well. Broken, flawed, and beautiful all at the same time.

He kissed her, and though they'd just finished, he already wanted her again.

CHAPTER ELEVEN

"Do you ever take a break?" Loki lounged on Val's bed, watching her dress.

"A break for what?" She slid her pants over her hips. She was considerably late returning to her shift.

He shrugged. "Anything fun."

Fun? She hadn't had fun in forever. "I beat the crap out of Odin. And we killed those demons on the way back."

"That's what you consider fun?"

She shrugged. "It's all the fun I've known for... forever."

She looked over Loki's perfect body. Man, she wished she didn't have to leave all seven feet of him lying there, naked like that, looking sexy as hel with his diamond colored eyes and taut, bluish frame. But she had a job and a responsibility, and she needed to keep her word.

"So, are you coming with me on Friday?" he asked.

Val stopped as she pulled her tank top over her head. "Friday?"

Loki rolled his eyes. "You know exactly what I'm talking about. Family dinner."

"How can you call all of them family after everything they've done to you and everything you've been through?"

Loki picked at her blanket for a minute. "Who else do I have? They are the only family I've known my whole life. They got me out of Valhalla. They helped me when I thought I would kill myself from boredom."

"That doesn't mean they are family. It means they are people who did you a favor. But can you really even call it a favor after all you've been through?" She pushed her feet into her boots.

Loki stood from the bed and wrapped her in his arms. "Please come with me."

She tried not to catch his eye. He didn't understand. Or maybe he did, she wasn't sure. She'd hated Odin and Thor for so long, she didn't know how to do or be anything else. She was sure that he'd never understand if she simply told him. He needed to see for himself.

She extricated herself from his grip and blew out a deep breath. She hadn't liked it when he'd done it the first time, and she damn sure she wouldn't like it this time, but it was the only way. For a moment, she wavered. She wasn't altogether sure what he would see. He could go anywhere he wanted… but she had told him she didn't want to hide from him. So… this was the biggest way to prove it. She held her hand out to him.

Loki looked at it. "You want to shake my hand? Wow. I don't think anyone has ever shaken my hand after a great round of sex."

She rolled her eyes. "No, dummy. I'm not trying to shake your hand. I'm offering you my hand."

His eyebrows smashed together. "You mean like marriage?"

She dropped her hand and shook her head. He could be so thick sometimes. She turned and headed to the door. "Never mind."

Loki caught her arm. "Wait."

She turned, and he watched her for a minute. "Oh. You mean, you're offering to let me do that thing that you said you'd kill me if I ever did again?"

Val swallowed hard. "Yes."

"But... why?"

"Because I need you to understand. Need you to see why I hate Odin and Thor so much. Words can't accurately describe it. I need you to see it."

Loki snapped his fingers, and his pants appeared low on his hips. "Are you sure?"

No. She sure as hel wasn't sure.

She nodded.

He pulled her hand into his and turned it palm up. He stroked down her palm several times before sucking in a deep breath and looking into her eyes. For a moment, she felt nothing, and then it happened. Like a movie playing in her mind.

Ripped away from her mother's embrace, she cried out, pleading for them to let her stay. Her mother's anguished sobs as she apologized over and over to her and promised to see her again. The scene changed. Days were filled with grueling training, not even big enough to lift her sword yet. Pushing her limits with every breath. Huddling together with her Valkyrie sisters, sobbing together, tending to each other's wounds, promising to be together forever, no matter what it took.

Countless battles across myriad worlds, their skies painted an otherworldly palette of swirling colors while the air echoed with the clash of steel and roars of anguished creatures. Thor doing Odin's bidding and then leaving them to find their dead sisters and bury them while he and his family and friends cheered and went off to drink and celebrate.

Odin sent them in, battle after battle, using them like paper towels sopping up the masses until he could come in and claim victory. And finally, the worst… Amidst Ragnarök's chaos, knowing the outcome, he refused to let them retreat. Refused to spare them. Refused to back down. Even Thor, in his arrogance, forced them to continue knowing it meant their deaths. And each of her sisters fell like petals in a storm until only she remained to shield Elle's mother.

The scene morphed. The harsh clatter of chains restricted her movements as gritty dirt shifted beneath her. The acrid stench of smoke mixed with fear during her relentless torture at Surtr's hands- His gravelly voice scraping over her in whispered promises of further torment. Until Elle's mother finally agreed to marry him, but only if he released Val.

Watching as Elle's mother consented to Surtr. Watching his abuse of her, but unable to do anything about it. Watching her grow sadder and weaker with every week of her pregnancy until the end, and the worst, most heartbreaking of all, when Elle's mother died.

When she couldn't handle any more, she pulled her hand away.

She cradled it close to her chest as if the memories had

wounded her, and she sucked in several deep breaths. The memories wracked her body as if she'd been there all over again. All of the death. The pain. The loss. She fought to keep it together when Loki's solid arms enveloped her.

"I'm so sorry, Signe. So very sorry." He kissed her head and held her tight against his torso.

She pushed from him gently and turned away, unable to handle his sympathy. She'd never shown anyone her pain before or talked about it with anyone, and she was conflicted about having done it.

"I have to head back to work." She brushed her hair behind her ear and walked to the door.

"Do you want to meet at Valhalla's Throne for tonight, or should I come get you?" Loki asked.

She stopped with her hand on the knob and blew out a breath. "I'll meet you there."

"Then I'll see you tonight." The sadness and pity in his voice were more than she could bear. She didn't need pity. Didn't need sympathy. She just needed him to understand. To understand and allow her her anger without trying to fix it.

She opened the door, but still couldn't gather up the courage to look back at him. "See you there."

She walked out the door and did exactly what she'd always told Elle to do. She held her head high, put back her shoulders, and refused to let anyone see her anguish.

Val strode down the stairs to the bar and found Frigg behind it. Crap. She'd been gone so long, Frigg had stepped in to bartend. That was not the kind of impression she wanted to make.

Val hurried to the bar and hopped over it. "I'm so sorry. I didn't mean to be gone that long."

Frigg smiled as she put two beers on a tray. "You've been working here for over a month and haven't even taken a full day off. I'm pretty sure I can forgive a few extra minutes on a lunch break."

Val gave her a tight smile. "Thank you."

She grabbed a towel from below the bar and began wiping it down when Frigg's hand landed on top of hers. Val stopped and looked into Frigg's beautiful, ageless face.

"Are you all right?"

Was she? No. Truly, she wasn't all right. Between things with Loki and the memories and taking care of Elle and having to meet the demon that night and having fought Odin, it was all... too much. Give her a sword and point her in a direction, and she could handle anything. But the emotional side of everything was just-

"I understand," said Frigg.

"You do?"

"I'm sorry for the pain the men in my family have caused you. And I know you are worried about Loki, but I can assure you he has nothing but good intentions toward you. I've never seen him care, truly care, for someone before."

Val opened her mouth, ready to pour out her soul, when Frigg looked over her shoulder, and Val turned as Loki descended the staircase, watching them.

Val nodded to Frigg and continued to wipe the bar. "Thank you for your words of comfort, Lady Frigg."

Without warning, Frigg stepped up to Val and pulled her

into a tight hug. "Your mother, Hogatha, would be so proud of the beautiful and strong woman you have become. But she would also want you to now follow your heart and find happiness at last."

Val froze. Frigg knew her mother? Knew her mother's name? A thousand questions swirled through her mind, but Frigg let go, kissed her forehead, and walked away.

Val couldn't move. Couldn't breathe.

"Val?"

Her head whipped up, and she peered at one of the waitresses.

"Are you okay?" she asked.

Val nodded and swallowed hard. "Yeah. Uh… what do you need?"

The girl rattled off the order for her table, and without thinking, Val turned and began gathering the ingredients for the drinks.

Her mother… Her mother's name was Hogatha.

"But where are you going?" Elle asked for the third time.

"I have some business to take care of." Val finished putting away the last of the glasses and checked the list on the wall behind the bar of things she needed to do before closing.

"What kind of business? You don't know anyone here besides me."

Val tried to keep her irritation in check. She had no interest in worrying Elle about Surtr, but she didn't want Elle trying to follow her down to Helheim either.

"I know lots of people. I know, Frigg, Loki, Thor, Odin, Heimdall-"

"Marek?"

"Right. I know Marek, too." She looked at the clock over the bar. "I gotta go."

"Are you staying up here or are you going down to Helheim?"

Val turned to her, needing to deflect the questions. "Why? Are you worried about me? Or are you checking to see where I'll be so you can sneak off and see Thor?"

Elle crossed her arms. "I don't need to sneak. I can see Thor if I want to."

Val nodded. "True. And I can go take care of my business if I want to. Just make sure you're in when I get back."

"When will that be?"

"I don't know, Grandma."

“Then how will I know when to be in by, Grandpa?”

Val stared at Elle, and then both of them broke into a smile. Val hadn't realized how much she'd missed Elle over the last few days. Elle rushed forward and hugged her. Val wrapped her arms around her friend and hugged her back. Neither moved for a second, and then Elle laughed.

"Wow."

"What?" asked Val.

"Whatever you are doing, or whomever you are doing it with, they must be pretty special."

"Why do you say that?"

"Because in the last two minutes you smiled and you hugged me. Like, really hugged me. Not one of those one-armed pats on the back you've always given me. You actually wrapped your arms around me and made full contact." Elle's eyes lit up.

"Shut up. I've hugged you before."

Elle shook her head. "You haven't. Not like you meant it. Maybe we should fight more often."

Val snorted. "Uh, how about we don't?"

"Do you promise to hug me again?"

Val couldn't help but laugh. Elle had always been able to lighten her spirits.

"I promise I will hug you again."

Elle nodded. "In the next month?"

"Don't push your luck."

Elle giggled and hugged Val again. "It is good to see you happy, Val. I worried so much that you would never be happy. I'm just wondering who is making you so happy."

Elle worried about her happiness? The concept was almost foreign to Val. She'd always been the one who took care of and worried about Elle. She'd never thought about Elle worrying about her.

"Ok. Ok. Let's not go mushy. I'm gonna be late." She patted Elle on the back.

Elle let go. "You... go do whatever it is you are doing. With whoever you are doing it with. And just know I will be here tonight. I'm gonna work on some of my jewelry. Maybe even make you something."

"I don't wear jewelry."

Elle shrugged. "You're changing. Maybe you'll finally wear some if I make it."

"Maybe. But don't get your hopes up."

Elle nodded. "Certainly not."

Val wished she didn't have to go. For the first time, she wanted to sit with Elle, talk to her, and hang out. They'd done so little of it since they'd been in Midgard. All the working and worrying had made Val beyond tense. And she'd not been able to relax enough to do anything... normal women might do. Not that there was anything normal about her. And not that she'd ever done any normal woman things… or even knew what they were.

"Go." Elle pushed her. "You don't want to keep Marek waiting."

Val headed for the portal. "It's not Marek."

"Okay, then... a hot demon."

Val waved, and her expression grew serious as she turned from Elle. Oh, it was a demon all right. But not a hot one- a dead one.

It surprised Val how easily she remembered the way to Valhalla's Throne, considering the fact that she hadn't paid attention when she and Loki had been walking there. But her feet carried her like they'd been there a million times. She stopped under the bright lights, tempted to go inside and buy a drink before the fight. She didn't have time, though. She had a job to do, and she needed to get it done. For Elle's sake, and her own.

She walked to the small darkened stairwell that led down to the fight ring and knocked on the door. The window opened, and Gadius peeked out.

"Hey," she said. "How are you? Do you remember me? I was here with Loki."

The cyclops nodded. "Yup. You beat Odin bad. That wasn't nice."

She nodded. "Right. Well, I have a match I'm supposed to fight in, so can you let me in?"

"Password?"

She scratched her head. "Uh... *Hjaldr.*"

"Sorry. Old word."

She thought they only changed it once a week. "I don't think Loki told me there was a new password, but he's the one who told me to come, so..."

"No password. No entrance. Sorry."

Val scratched her head. "Okay, well, can you tell me if Loki is in there?"

"I can't tell you that."

She nodded. "How about this? You go ask Loki if I can come in. I'll wait here."

"What if he isn't in here?"

"He told me to meet him here, so I guess I'll wait for him to show up and let me in himself."

Gadius' eyebrow creased like he was thinking hard. Then he nodded once and closed the window.

Val looked around and leaned against the wall. Loki hadn't specified an actual time, so it was possible he hadn't arrived. Either way, she'd find him and his client and take care of what needed to be done to ensure Elle's freedom and safety.

It was less than five minutes before the door to the fight club swung inward, and Loki stepped out.

He shook his head. "Have you been waiting long? Lunkhead just told me you were out here."

"A few minutes."

He kissed her cheek. "Good thing you told him to look for me, or you could have been out here all night."

"Hopefully not all night. I'd like to think you would have come looking for me at some point."

"Of course. So, are you going to do this?"

She nodded. "I need to talk to the guy first, though."

"That shouldn't be a problem."

"Then let's get this over with."

Loki led her down the hallway to the ring. The crowd was much larger than it had been before.

"Tonight's a full roster," Loki said.

She wondered how many people would bet on her again and how many would lose. Even though she didn't know what the outcome was going to be, one thing was for sure- she refused to let the demon take Elle back to Surtr. No matter what she had to do.

"Let's sit over there." Loki pointed to a high section in a darker area of the arena.

They pushed past the cheering crowd and headed to the empty bench on the other side of the room. She could only figure that Loki had walked them all the way around, so whoever they were supposed to meet saw them and decided if they were going to talk to her.

They sat on the wooden bench, and Loki leaned in. "Do you want a drink?"

She nodded and held up two fingers. He squeezed her knee, walked down the bench, and out of a curtain between rows. She watched the fight for a minute, analyzing the fighters and their moves.

One of the fighters had close to a hundred pounds on the other, but he was slow and sloppy. The smaller fighter used the first's weight to his advantage. He moved around the ring, making the larger fighter expend all of his energy chasing him. Val grew bored and looked away. It was obvious the way the fight would play out. The big guy would tire, and then the little one would go in for the knockout. Not a bad strategy. Probably what she would have done.

"I take it you're the Valkyrie," said a smooth, low voice from the darkness.

Val swung around and looked at what appeared to be a blank wall. A form emerged from the shadows and sat next to her. She stared at him for a moment. He was nothing like what she'd expected. She'd expected a big, burly, menacing type of demon, maybe wearing leather and bondage gear, maybe wearing very little. He wasn't, though. He was a soft-skinned, well-tailored young man who looked like he'd stepped out of a fashion shoot. Not a hair on his head stood out of place. His age was indeterminable, but if she saw him on Midgard, she would have guessed he was no more than a late teen or early twenties.

"I take it from your silence I'm correct." The demon turned his orange eyes on her.

"And your name?" she asked.

He shrugged. "Is that really necessary?"

"You know me, but I don't know you. I'm not going to make a deal with someone who won't even tell me who he is."

He chuckled. "I was told you had spirit."

She wondered who had told him that. Loki? Or Surtr?

He looked at the fight. "My name is Alamax."

"Why do all you demons have names that end in -ax?"

He smiled, revealing sharp, long canines. "I don't know, honestly. I guess it's kind of like humans who name all their kids' names that start with the same letter."

"What did Surtr promise you?" she asked.

His gaze slid sideways toward her. "Are you going to offer me more?"

"No. I just wondered what I was worth."

"Technically, you are only half the pay day that your friend is."

"She's off the table."

"That's not what I agreed to-"

"I don't care what you agreed to. You either make a deal for me and me alone, or we don't make a deal."

He looked at her again, and a grin slid across his face. "I don't have to make a deal at all. I can just take you now."

Val pulled out a knife and held it to his throat faster than he could blink. "I think not."

His gaze never broke contact with hers. "To be honest, I love a good street fight, but this is my favorite suit, and I would hate to ruin it. So, what are you proposing?"

"We fight. In the cage. You win, you take me and only me, back to Surtr and collect whatever he will give you for me."

"And if you win?"

"You tell Surtr we aren't here. That you've looked everywhere and checked all your contacts on Midgard as well as in the Underworld, and no one has seen us."

He chewed his lip for a minute, and for a second she thought a twinkle sparkled in his eyes. "I can live with that," he finally said.

She nodded. "Then let's do this."

He unbuttoned his jacket, and everyone broke into cheers in the audience as the large man in the cage fell backward on the mat, unconscious.

"Just one more fight and then we're up," said Alamax.

Val nodded. "I'd say good luck, but to be honest, I don't want you to have any."

Alamax's smile widened. "You know, if you weren't a contract, I'd ask you to dinner."

"Sorry, I can't say the same." Val turned back to the fight as Gadius entered the ring and dragged the larger man out. Alamax stood and disappeared back into the darkness.

Loki approached and handed her a drink. "Did you talk to him?"

"Yup. Our fight is coming up soon." She downed her drink and then took his second one and downed it as well.

"Wait, what?" Loki looked at her.

"What, what?" she asked. "That's why you got me here, right? For us to fight?"

"Well... yes, but I thought you were going to try and talk him out of fighting and into something else."

“Like what? Sex? No, thank you.”

He growled. “That's not what I meant.”

She stared at him. "Good. Though offering you up to him wasn't off the list.”

He frowned, making her chuckle.

“I'm kidding. I'd never let him have you. And not fighting was never my plan."

"Then what did you need to talk to him about?" The strain in Loki's voice grew intense.

She wasn't sure she wanted to tell him the deal she'd made. Mostly because if Loki knew what she'd agreed to, he would try to stop it any way possible. But she didn't want to stop it.

She'd made a promise to protect Elle, and if that meant she needed to sacrifice herself to keep her safe, then that's what she needed to do. No matter the cost to herself. No matter what Surtr might do to her. No matter that it meant she would have to leave Loki behind. The only person she'd ever... loved? No. She'd loved people before. Just... not the way she loved him. Shit. Did she love him? He'd said he loved her. And in that moment, she realized that she did love him. How the hel had that happened? When had it happened? They'd known each other for less than a week!

"We talked about the terms of the fight. As you said, if he wins, he gets his ransom. If he loses, he tells Surtr we aren't here."

Loki studied her face for deceit. He wouldn't find any. What she'd told him was the truth… technically.

The bell rang on the match at hand, and Val turned to look in the cage. Damn. The last fight hadn't even lasted five minutes. She'd hoped to have a bit more time with Loki before her possible relocation back to Muspelheim.

"Guess that means I'm up." She downed the second drink and stood, stretching her arms. A twitch of fear skittered over her, but she shoved it down like bile. She was not scared of Frat Boy, Alamax.

She reached into her boots and removed her knives, handing them to Loki. He looked at them and placed them inside his jacket. She reached for her blade on her back, but he stopped her and shook his head.

"Not that one. Keep that one. In case you need it."

"Isn't that against the rules?"

"I know, love, but I'll be honest. I hadn't expected you to

fight him. I thought you would use your unnerving charm to make some kind of a different deal."

"Unnerving charm? We've met before, right?"

Loki stood and cupped her face. "You can't trust Alamax. He may not use any powers, but that doesn't mean he'll play fair. He's known to do whatever it takes to get what he wants."

She scanned his face. "You don't think I can beat him."

"I didn't say that."

"Then what are you saying?"

He blew out a breath and then kissed her. "I'm saying if anything happens to you, I wouldn't want to exist anymore."

Her chest squeezed. She closed her eyes and lay her forehead on his. What did she say to that?

She blew out a breath of her own and said, "Then I'd better win."

Loki looked at her, and his eyes turned ice blue. "I won't let him take you and Elle. Thor won't either. No matter what deal you made with him, he didn't make a deal with us."

"That's not exactly fair. Aren't you worried about your clientele?"

"I don't give a crap about my clients. I'm not losing you."

"And Lucifer?"

"Would you go to Valhalla and raise hel with me?"

She chuckled. "As long as I don't have to fan you all day and bring you ale and shit."

"Well, you're not a virgin, so I don't think you have to worry about that."

She punched him in the gut.

He grimaced. "I wasn't complaining."

"Val, you're up," Gadius called.

Val nodded and kissed Loki. "I got this."

"I'll be waiting right here. Well, no. Actually, I'll be right down there at the edge of the cage making sure you are okay."

"Sounds good. Just promise me one thing."

"What's that?"

"No matter what happens, you won't stop the match."

"Signe-"

"Promise me, Loki." Her voice came out stronger than she'd anticipated.

Loki sucked in a breath and nodded. "I promise."

She gave him a tight smile and then turned and headed down to the cage. Alamax already stood in the middle of the ring. Shirtless and in nothing but workout shorts and bare feet. She wondered what his fighting skills consisted of.

Val ascended the stairs into the cage and walked to the middle opposite Alamax.

"I want you to know I'll take no pleasure in hurting you," he said. "I'm not that kind of demon."

"Don't stress it. I'm going to take a lot of pleasure in kicking your ass."

He shook his head. "I really wish I were taking you out instead of taking you to Surtr."

"Again, don't stress it. I'm spoken for anyway." Why the hel had she told him that?

His eyebrows rose. "Really? Anyone I know?"

"Are we fighting or chatting like long-distance sisters?" Val steadied herself, her muscles tensed as she faced off against Alamax. Dark energy swirled around him, a chilling presence that sent shivers down her spine.

He smiled, revealing his pointed teeth, and didn't give Val

a chance to prepare before he leaped forward and kicked her in the gut, sending her flying into the cage wall and dropping to the floor, winded.

So that's what Loki meant by he fought dirty. Fair enough.

Val pushed to her hands and knees as he plummeted next to her and kicked her in the stomach again. Val rolled over and hopped to her feet, trying desperately to suck in a breath. But Alamax wasn't going to give her a chance. With another burst of speed, Alamax lunged forward and aimed a swift kick at Val's midsection. She deftly twisted to the side, narrowly evading the blow. She retaliated with a fierce jab, aiming for his exposed ribs. The impact reverberated through her arm as she made contact, but Alamax barely flinched.

Damn. He moved as fast as any enemy she'd ever fought. He swung at her, and Val released her wings, shredding yet another shirt, and rose two feet above his head, giving her time to gulp down air.

Alamax looked up at where she hovered and smiled. "In the air works too."

Black feathery wings sprouted from his back, and he met her where she hovered.

A fallen angel. Alamax was a fallen angel. Damn. That explained a lot.

Again, he didn't give her a moment to recover, and instead, he charged her. She spun out of the way and kicked him in the back. He smashed face-first into the cage, bounced off, and flew straight at her, fist raised. Val launched into a flurry of strikes and kicks, each movement calculated and precise. Muscle memory kept her moving without having to think. All the decades of battles flowed back through her like she'd been through them the day before.

Alamax countered with equal skill, their bodies moving in a deadly dance of combat. The fight intensified as they circled each other, their movements fluid and controlled. Val ducked under Alamax's sweeping punch and spun around, delivering a punishing kick to his side. Before he could react, Val closed the distance between them and unleashed a rapid series of strikes, her blows landing with unrelenting force. Alamax grunted in pain, his defenses faltering under her relentless assault. He tried to spin away, but grabbed his wing and slammed her fist into his joint. He cried out as the wing retracted and he dropped to the floor of the arena.

The crowd erupted in cheers. Even Loki yelled her name, but she didn't have time to think about him.

She dove down and landed where he should have been, but he'd disappeared and reappeared on the opposite side of the arena.

"Cheat!" someone yelled. "No magic allowed."

"Cheat," someone else cried out. "Forfeit. He forfeits."

No. She couldn't let him. She had to win on her own. He'd never keep his word if he were forced to forfeit.

"No," she yelled. "I can still beat him. No forfeiting."

"But no more magic, either," yelled Loki. He flicked his fingers at Alamax, and silvery bands laced up Alamax's arms.

"You can't bind me. Then it's not a fair fight."

"I'm only binding your magic. Nothing more." Loki looked over his shoulder, and Val followed his gaze to see Odin sitting in his chair.

When had he gotten there?

"I'll allow it," Odin declared. "The magic binding stays. If you try to cheat again, you'll deal with me."

Alamax's eyes blazed with golden fury as he turned back on Val and raced forward. She went to roll away, but he caught her leg and yanked her back before kicking her in the gut again.

Her drinks from earlier threatened to come back up, but she refused to allow them. While on all fours, he lifted her head and slammed her nose into his knee. Blood gushed from her face, splattering the ground.

Loki roared behind her. "I'm going to kill you!"

Alamax laughed. "Guess I know who you belong to."

Val fought against the pain skyrocketing through her skull and got to her feet, grabbing him by the balls.

His eyes bulged out, and his mouth opened in a silent scream.

"I belong to no one." She slammed her fist into the side of his head, dropping him to the ground, but he staggered to his feet as she wiped the blood from her face and spat on the floor. Val's focus narrowed to a laser-sharp point as she pushed herself to the limit. She needed to end this.

Val delivered a decisive blow, sending Alamax crashing into the cage wall again. She advanced and punched him over and over. Face. Gut. Shoulder. Kidney. Other kidney.

Alamax struggled to keep up with her relentless onslaught, his once-confident facade crumbling under the weight of her determination.

He cried out as she grabbed one of his wings and yanked it backward, snapping it. He shuddered, and his wings retracted as he crumbled to the ground and curled into a ball, but Val refused to let up. She kicked him with her heavy boot. He kicked out with his legs trying to trip her, but she lifted off the ground, and he missed. He rolled on his back, and she dropped onto his chest. The cracks that emanated told her she'd broken his sternum, collarbone, and ribs with one brutal stroke. Alamax screamed and fought to suck in a shallow breath, but couldn't.

"You're not like any opponent I've faced before," he admitted.

Val knelt over him, her fist above his face. "Concede and tell Surtr you couldn't find us."

Alamax coughed up blood. "I've never once not fulfilled a contract," he choked out.

"I can keep beating you until you pass out, but I'm giving you the opportunity to save face."

He tried to laugh but ended up coughing and spitting blood. "You think throwing in the towel is going to help me save face? You don't know the kinds of beings I work with. The only way for me to save face is for you to knock me out. Killing me would be better."

She shrugged. "If that's what you wish."

"Just so you know, I'll tell Surtr I couldn't find you. But that doesn't mean one of my siblings won't go to him and make a deal."

Rage erupted inside her. "You promised-"

"That I wouldn't tell him. I can't say the same for my siblings. I have a lot of them. And we're all in the bounty hunting business."

Val's mind reeled. What did she do? They had a deal, but he was breaking it. Loki had told her not to trust him, and she should have listened. Her fists rained down on Alamax like thunder from above. Over and over, she punched him in the face. He tried in vain to push her off and to protect himself from her blows, but he'd become too weak.

"Tell me you'll keep the deal and make sure your siblings do the same," she shouted.

Alamax laughed, choking on his own blood as she continued to pummel him. Finally, he stopped laughing, and his eyes rolled back in his head.

She shook his shoulders. "Keep your end of the bargain. Keep your end!"

Loki ran into the cage. "What's going on?"

"He lied. He said he wouldn't tell Surtr if I won. But now he said he couldn't promise his siblings would do the same."

Loki lifted her to her feet.

She peered up into his face, her body a cacophony of rage, pain, and fear. "What the hel good was all this if we are still going to be hunted?"

"I'll take care of it."

"How?" she demanded. "How are you going to take care of it? Do you want me to fight all of his siblings?"

"No," Loki said in a calm voice. "You made a deal with him, and he has to keep it. It's possible his siblings don't know about the contract. It's not like they are all shary shary. I'll talk to them. I'll take care of it. I promise. All right?"

She nodded as the cyclops entered, grabbed Alamax by his arm, and dragged him out of the arena.

"I gotta get out of here," she said. "I just... I can't..."

"Come on," he said. "I know what you need."

She groaned. "Not this time. I'm too angry."

Loki led her away by the hand. “That’s not what I had in mind.”

He headed straight for the exit and stepped out onto the darkened street.

"Where are we going?" she asked.

Loki looked at her and winked. "My place."

CHAPTER TWELVE

Loki's fury at Alamax's trying to take advantage of Val was almost too much for him to contain. He wanted to go back, find the fallen angel, and cut his head off for lying. No. Cutting his head off would be too easy. He wanted to make Alamax suffer. Suffer the way Loki had suffered by being chained to a rock, having his entrails eaten, and acid dripping on him.

But he couldn't do that. So, he'd have to do things the more prudent way. With money.

That would have to wait until tomorrow morning. At the moment, he had a more important promise to fulfill. He needed to take care of Val.

He poured two ales in his stark white kitchen and walked from his modern, spotless white-and-cream living room. The home remained pale as the day he'd moved in. White walls, cream upholstered sofas, a bleached oak coffee table centered on a wool rug, the color of old bone. Every surface sanitized, deliberately anonymous, the kind of space that belonged to no one. At least, that's what others would think if he ever had people over, which he didn't. Aside from his son Fenrir and, on one occasion, his daughter Hel, he'd never had anyone to his place before. Not even his other children had been there. Not that he was in contact with them. Being more beast than anything, they'd been unaffected by the destruction of Asgard, since they'd never lived there anyway.

He barely spent any time in his house himself, to be honest. Mostly because it never felt like a home, just a place to crash, wash, and store his things. Floor-to-ceiling windows overlooked the large balcony where Val stood, wings spread, letting the air blow through her hair. A car alarm wailed, then cut out. He walked through one of the large sliding glass doors to the balcony that overlooked all of Los Angeles.

"This is amazing," Val said, setting the bag of ice he'd given her on the railing. Her eyes sported deep bruises underneath them, but at least her nose wasn't crooked, and her cheekbones had been spared any blows. The sight of her so beaten made his gut clench, and he gripped his mug of ale tighter. Alamax was definitely no longer a client. And the first chance he got, Loki was going to invite that asshole to challenge him at Valhalla's Throne. Val had beaten him, but Loki planned on destroying him.

Loki handed her the mug of ale. "Thank you. I like that I see all of the city but still feel like I have my own space."

"Yes, that is quite amazing. I had no idea that these hills had houses on them. Surrounded by the forest makes it feel like your own private kingdom."

"I can do whatever I want up here, and no one bothers me."

She sipped the ale. "Whatever you want, huh? And what type of 'whatever' have you done up here?"

His gaze slid to hers, and he caught the faintest smile on her lips. "I've walked around naked in the house."

She rolled her eyes. "Hasn't everyone?"

"I've done yoga out here naked."

She shrugged. "Better."

Ooohhhh, a challenge. "I've flown through the trees during a full moon to watch the shifters run."

"Wait. You've flown up here?"

That caught her attention. "Many times."

"And no one sees you?"

He shrugged. "If they have, they've never said anything. Not that I even know my neighbors. That's the thing about living up here. People do it for the nature, but they also do it because they want to be left alone, and they expect everyone else to do the same."

"So, I can fly up here?" Her eyes held a gleam he'd not seen in them before. Something between childlike happiness and hope.

"Of course. It's one of the reasons I brought you. If you think you're well enough to fly. You took quite a beating tonight."

Val downed her ale and began to strip off her layers. "As long as my wings work, every other bone in my body could be broken, and I would still want to fly."

Damn, he liked her... no... he loved her. The thought

struck him as hard as when he'd said it out loud to her. Loki stripped down to his pants. "Then let's go."

They took to the sky, and it was like a century vanished from Val's demeanor. It took her a few minutes to warm up her wings and get back into the rhythm of flying, but once she had, there was no stopping her. She flew higher and faster than Loki would have imagined. He followed closely but gave her the space she needed to maneuver without being crowded by him.

Loki had seen thousands of creatures fly in his lifetime, but watching Val brought him a happiness and sense of peace that radiated through him. She glided gracefully high above the clouds, dipping down and turning suddenly into a death spiral, only to stop and immediately fly straight up again, bursting through the clouds like a rocket.

They flew for close to half an hour when he noticed her begin to fatigue. He raced to where she lazily flew in and out of sight.

"I think you should rest," he called.

She looked back at him. "I could fly like this forever."

"I'm sure in your heart you can, but what about your wings? They aren't used to being used so much. We don't want them to get sore or pull something. Let's go back, and I'll massage them for you."

She dipped down into the clouds, and he waited a moment for her to reemerge, but she didn't. In a slight panic, he spun in a circle, and she came up behind him and jumped on his back, wrapping her arms around his neck.

"You'll massage my wings?" She nipped his neck, making him shiver.

"I'll massage any part you want me to."

She licked up the side of his throat, and he reached back and grabbed her rear.

"Signe-"

"Loki."

Her warm breath hit his bare skin, and he wanted nothing more than to take her right there.

"Do you think we could make love up here?" she asked.

Damn, that was tempting. "I think we could, up until we both climax and get lost in each other and plummet to our deaths."

"Mmmmm… but it would be an amazing death."

He sighed. "Glorious."

She bit his shoulder and let go of him. He spun as she flew backward, grabbed her hand, and pulled her to him. She wrapped her wings around him, and he kissed her soft.

"Thank you," she said.

Whoa! First smiles and now a thank you? "For what?"

"Everything. Helping me fight Odin. Finding out who is hunting us. This."

He almost exploded from pleasing her as if somehow it had become the most important thing in his long life. "You are most welcome, love."

She wrapped her arms around his neck. "I just ask one thing."

He kissed her again. "Anything."

She chewed her lip for a moment. "If you regret anything you've said to me, or done with me, or have had second thoughts of any kind, that you be honest with me and tell me now."

He took in her beautiful face. She was scared. It shone in her eyes. Did that mean she felt for him what he felt for her? What other reason would she have for being scared?

He ran his knuckles over her cheek. "The only thing I regret is that I didn't get to spend my first millennium with you."

Tears flooded her eyes. "You're cheesy, you know that?"

He smiled. "But you love that about me, don't you?"

"Maybe."

"And you love me as well."

A tear tumbled down her cheek. "Gods know I didn't want to, but you just… got under my skin somehow, and now when I'm not with you, it's like an itch I can't scratch."

"Are you saying I'm irritating?"

She kissed him. "Absolutely. And I simply love you for it."

Loki snapped his fingers, and they were in his bedroom, kissing and throwing off their clothes as fast as they were able.

When he entered her, she pulled away. "Wait."

"What's wrong?"

"I want you, Loki of the *Jötunn*."

It was his turn to be scared. "Are you sure?"

"I love you. Not the façade you show everyone else. The real you. So like I've told you before, I want you to be the real you with me, always, every time we are alone."

His heart beat so fast he thought it might go into arrest. He dropped his magic and let the shroud that always covered him fall away like a scarf in the wind. His body lengthened, and his skin darkened against her peachiness.

She stroked his face. "Make love to me, Loki."

He didn't need to be asked twice. He kissed her and poised

at her entrance. Excruciatingly slowly, he slid inside her inch by inch. The feel of his real skin on her skin was enough to almost tumble him over the edge. It was nothing like having sex with his façade on. It was a thousand times more sensational. Every fiber of him lit up as if his whole life he'd been having sex while wearing a woolen blanket.

He couldn't hold back the moan that escaped him as he leaned in and bit her lip.

She grabbed his rear and urged him for more.

Loki took it slow. Savoring every sense as if it were his first time. "I… I…" He couldn't form words.

"What's wrong?" she asked.

"I've never had sex without the façade before you, and it just… the way you feel…"

She kissed him and pushed him onto his back. "Is it different?"

"It's a completely new experience. Everything is so much more. I can't explain it."

A glint sparked in her eyes, and she flipped him over and slid down on him in one fluid movement. He grabbed her hips and arched off the bed. Her tight body wrapped around his had him so close to losing it.

"I… I won't be able to hold out," he panted.

She leaned in and bit his bottom lip. "Who said you had to?"

She grabbed his horns and held on as she bucked her hips into his. She was touching him. Touching him and making love to him. Him. The bastard *Jötunn*. The outcast. The loner. And from the look of it, she wasn't faking her pleasure.

"Signe… my love."

She rocked her hips into his and pulled harder on his horns, almost making him sit up. The sensation of her hands on his horns had tingles skittering over his entire body until his climax slammed into him so hard he lost all thought. Pleasure. Pain. Joy. All of them mixed together in a blur as he stared at her beautiful face.

"Signe…" His body wound so tight he couldn't breathe and shook with pleasure as his climax went on and on for what seemed like a lifetime and then tapered off.

When he was able to breathe again, he grabbed her head and kissed her so hard his teeth ached. But he didn't care. He wanted her. Needed her. And she was his. He'd never let Alamax or anyone else take her from him. Whatever it took. He would never give her up.

When he broke this kiss, she smiled. He pulled her into his chest and clung to her for several minutes before realizing she hadn't climaxed.

"I am so sorry, love. I didn't get you there."

She sat up. "This isn't about me."

"It's always about you. It always will be. I promised to take care of you after the fight."

"And you will. But right now what I want is to give you a first you won't ever forget."

His eyebrows rose. "Really?"

She kissed his lips and then his collarbone. Each nipple. His side. His hip. And then further down between his legs.

"Yes." She swirled her tongue around the tip of him, and he grabbed the sheets to keep from bucking off the bed.

"Signe."

She slid her tongue down his length. "Loki."

He threw his head back as waves of pleasure radiated out through him. "You're going to be the death of me, woman."

She chuckled. "As long as you are all mine, you can keep telling me that."

She licked back up his shaft and took him into her mouth.

Loki swore in Gaelic and sank into the bed as she sucked him into oblivion.

CHAPTER THIRTEEN

Friday afternoon rolled around, Val received a text from Loki telling her he'd be there to pick her up around six thirty. Her stomach roiled, and she took a deep breath to keep from throwing up. He hadn't asked her since the last time she'd told him no, but that had been two days ago. A lot had changed between them in that time.

Val stared at the text, trying to figure out how to cancel having to go to Odin's. Out of the corner of her eye, she spotted the black box Loki had given her. She hadn't touched it since she'd put it on the shelf, but curiosity suddenly pulled her to it like a magnet. She stared at it for a long minute, trying to work up the nerve to take a peek. Whatever it was would probably be ridiculously expensive, flashy, and way too small for her. Even so, she couldn't help but be intrigued.

She looked at the clock. "I'm taking my break," she announced before grabbing the box and heading to her apartment.

Once inside, she set the box on the table and stepped back. Her mind raced with what might be inside. She'd never once worn a dress before, and the fanciest thing she'd ever worn was her ceremonial battle armor to official events.

Her fingers twitched the longer she stared at the box, and finally she flipped the lid off it and took a step back, as if it might bite her.

Her eyes widened, and she couldn't help but step forward again. She ran her fingers over the champagne-colored silk, then lifted it from the box and held it up.

The dress fell to her knee, and she took in the whole of it. A halter top dress, with a jeweled collar and jeweled chains that draped down over the shoulders like pauldrons- but completely useless in battle, obviously. She turned it around to find the back cut out, but surprisingly, it was neither low-cut in the front nor so short her lady bits would show, unlike a lot of dresses women wore into the bar. It was sexy without being overly revealing.

The jeweled collar and chains sparkled so bright she wondered if they were made of real diamonds.

She laid the dress on the table and stepped back again. She wanted to try it on more than anything, but she didn't want the stench of beer and sweat on it. She looked in the mirror again. Her bruises had all but healed, so there was no using them or pain as an excuse to say no. She looked at the dress again. It really was gorgeous. And she couldn't help the desire to have Loki see her in it.

She grabbed her phone and texted three words.

See you then.

At five thirty, Val walked up to her apartment and showered. She pulled on the only pair of sexy underwear she owned and skipped the bra. She slipped into the dress. The fabric slid over her like a second skin, only softer and smoother. She clasped the jeweled collar, and for a moment, a shiver of panic raced through her as it reminded her of the collar Surtr had put on her when she'd first gotten to Muspelheim. She swallowed down the memory and reminded herself she was in Midgard and safe.

She blew out a deep breath before turning to look in the mirror, unable to move for several seconds. She was… a woman. Of course, she was a woman, but in that dress, she actually felt like a woman. A real woman. Not a soldier. Not a protector. Just… a woman. She'd never been just a woman before. Every second of her life had been spent in service to someone else, but for once, she was going out and doing something she wanted to do. Wearing something she chose. With no restriction. No rules. No one telling her what to do. The idea thrilled and scared her.

Free… she really was free.

She grabbed her brush and ran through her long hair, ready to put it up in a ponytail, but instead she let it fall down her back. Between her golden curls and the champagne and diamond dress, she looked like an angel she'd seen in a book once. For a moment, she wondered what Alamax had looked like as an angel. Probably Cupid or some other cherub-looking thing.

She smiled at her reflection and quickly covered her mouth. She'd never smiled at herself before. She removed her hand and smiled again. The expression felt strange on her face, but she had to admit she liked how she looked- and how it felt. As if it were natural, something she always did. Was this her life now? Her new normal? Where she dressed in fancy dresses, let her hair hang down, and smiled when she saw herself? She couldn't imagine her life being like that from now on. She dared not even hope… yet some place deep inside her longed for it. Longed to be able to be free, and love, and be loved.

A knock sounded on the door, and she glanced at the time. It was only six fifteen. Loki was punctual, but he wouldn't be early. Unless he was checking to make sure she was actually getting ready.

She walked to the door and pulled it open, ready to give Loki an earful when she stopped.

"Evening, Valkyrie."

"Heimdall." She scanned the hallway to see if anyone else was around. "Can I help you?"

He held out a box. Val looked at it and then at Heimdall.

"Frigg said you wouldn't have any shoes, and if you didn't have shoes, then you wouldn't go to family dinner. So she bought you some."

Val looked at the box and took it from Heimdall. "Uh… thank you." She hadn't thought about shoes. Of course, she didn't have shoes that would go with a fancy dress. All she had were boots and sneakers.

Heimdall nodded and turned to go, but stopped and turned back. He looked her up and down for a minute before meeting her eyes again.

"You look lovely," he said, before continuing down the hallway.

"Uh… thank you?" Really? The demi-god brought her a pair of shoes and told her she looked lovely. Was that all she could think to say? "Will I see you at the dinner?"

He paused. "Not tonight. But soon."

Okay... "Have a good night, Heimdall."

He waved over his shoulder but didn't turn as he headed down the stairs and out of sight.

Val read the brand on the box and noticed music coming from Elle's room. Her door stood open a crack, and Val approached it.

Inside, Elle sang along to the popular music they played in the bar. She listened for a minute and smiled. She took a moment to enjoy Elle's beautiful voice before the music shut off and Elle pulled open the door.

She let out a little scream.

"Sorry," said Val. "I was just listening. I've always loved your voice."

Elle smiled so bright Val thought she might crack her face. She looked over Elle in an expensive green dress. Seems she wasn't the only one receiving expensive gifts from Norse gods.

"Are you going out?" Val asked.

Elle nodded. "I was invited to a party at Odin's house."

Val's stomach plummeted, of course. Loki had told her that Elle would be invited. "You know it's not a party, right? It's a family dinner. All of Thor's family will be there. All of them."

Elle's eyebrows scrunched together. "So?"

"So…" Val looked down the hallway and then pushed into Elle's apartment, closing the door most of the way. "You know what, so."

"I don't understand-"

"You do. You are just choosing not to listen to me. I understand you have feelings for Thor, and that's something I am coming to terms with, but his whole family? There is going to be someone there who figures out who you are."

"I don't care anymore." She crossed her arms over her chest.

"Will Thor? I'm assuming you still haven't told him."

"I'm going to. Tonight. Right after dinner."

Val shook her head. "You should tell him before dinner."

"Why? Because you don't want me to go?"

Val didn't answer.

"Why are you trying to ruin this for me?" Fire lit Elle's eyes.

Val needed to try a new tactic before Elle lost her temper, and something unfortunate happened.

"I'm not. It's just… dangerous down there. People are looking for us. Hunting us."

"How do you know? Have you seen them? Heard of them?" Fear tinged Elle's words.

Val's gut twisted. There were more beings hunting them than she wanted to admit, but she refused to worry Elle. Telling her the truth would keep her from going to the family dinner, but… then Val would feel guilty for going herself. And for the first time, Val really did want to do something. Something with Loki. And wearing the dress he'd bought her.

"No," Val lied. "I just know Surtr, and he won't let us go. He has to be looking for us."

"Well, if he hasn't found us, and you haven't heard

anything, then I'm going. And I promise I'll tell Thor after family dinner."

Val shook her head. "I'm telling you, this isn't a good idea."

"Why?" Elle asked. "Thor and his entire family will be there."

"Exactly."

"I can't be safer anywhere in the Underworld than with the entire family of Norse gods in Helheim."

Val glowered at her. "That's not what I mean."

"I can't be afraid forever, Val. You brought me here to have a life. That's what I'm doing. Would you rather I fell for a demon or something else?"

"Of course not, it's just-"

"What? You'll be there too, I assume." Elle looked Val up and down.

Val was losing the fight, and without telling Elle the truth, there was nothing that was going to stop her.

A knock sounded on the door, and it swung inward. Thor stood in the doorway. How much had he heard? Obviously, not everything from his relaxed demeanor.

Val eyed him for a moment and then strode from the room, stomped down the hall, and headed down the stairs to the bar. She scanned the room, and dozens of eyeballs landed on her, making her blush. She hurried to Heimdall's booth and slid in.

His eyes widened. "Valkyrie."

"I'm…" she sighed. "I don't know what I am doing, actually."

"I would say you are hiding with a side helping of running away."

She chuckled. "That's a nice way of putting it."

She took the shoes out of the box without looking at them and slid them onto her feet.

"What do I do?" she asked, setting the box under the table.

Heimdall shrugged.

"Come on," she said. "Don't be like that.

"Valkyrie, you more than anyone should know that no matter what I tell you, it won't change what is going to happen."

"Then tell me what is going to happen so I can be prepared."

He shook his head.

She swore several times and shook her head. "You know, Heimdall, you can be a real pain in the ass, but I respect the hel out of you for all you do and see and put up with."

For the first time, she spotted real emotion in Heimdall's golden eyes, and he gave her a soft smile.

"Thank you, Signe, daughter of Hogatha and Leif."

Wait what? Her father's name was Leif? A million questions swarmed through her mind, but Heimdall's expression told her he wasn't going to give her more.

Loki walked up the stairs, and Val's full attention turned to him. Dark blue suit cut to fit him amazingly. Hair pulled back in a slick ponytail at the base of his neck. Scruff enough to tickle her skin and give his beautiful face a more rugged appearance. Suddenly, she didn't want to go to the family dinner. All she wanted was to strip his suit from him and make love to him all night long.

"You should go," said Heimdall.

She nodded without looking at him and stood. She wobbled for a moment as the heels she'd put on twisted underneath her, but as she was about to lose her balance, a strong arm wrapped around her waist and kept her upright. She slammed into Loki's chest and looked up to find his eyes lit like diamonds.

He smiled, and his eyes took in every inch of her face. "Hello, future wife."

What? "Hello, possible husband."

Loki set Val back on her feet, his gaze sweeping over the exquisite fit of her dress. It shimmered like starlight against her skin, hugging her figure in effortless elegance. Her hair cascaded past her shoulders and flowed like a silken river down her back, every strand inviting his touch.

"Hello, future wife." The words slipped out before he could catch them.

Her eyes widened as the corners of her lips curved into a teasing grin. "Hello, possible husband."

A smile tugged at Loki's lips. "Possible, huh? I guess I'll have to work harder to get you."

Despite a desire to whisk her away with a thought and tumble them both into the privacy of his bedsheets, he refrained.

The bar's usual murmur had quieted, fading under lusty glances drawn by Val's presence like moths to candles. Male gazes lingered too long for Loki's comfort- a mortal error if ever there was one.

With deliberate possessiveness, Loki tangled his fingers through her hair and drew her closer until their mouths met. Her lips parted, inviting him in, her breath hot against his mouth like a promise.

Loki didn't ask. He took.

Her arms encircled him, fingertips trailing across the expanse of his back as she kissed him without hesitation or care for prying eyes around them.

His fingers tugged her hair hard enough to make her gasp. He swallowed the sound greedily, his tongue sliding against hers. She tasted like mint and something sweet, something hers, and he wanted to drown in it. Her hands clawed at his back, nails digging through his suit jacket, and he groaned into her mouth, grinding his hips forward just to feel her shudder against him.

The bar around them blurred into nothing- just heat, and her. The slide of their tongues, the scrape of her teeth against his bottom lip, the way she arched into him like she couldn't stand even an inch of space between them. His other hand dropped to her waist, fingers digging into soft flesh, dragging her closer until he felt every curve of her pressed against him.

In that moment, they crafted their own world. A realm where all else dimmed away but each other.

Someone cleared their throat to his left and then said, "They get the point. You can stop now."

Damned Heimdall.

Loki didn't stop. He kissed Val for another few seconds before kissing her nose and pulling her into a hug.

He glanced around the bar again, and the men turned their jealous eyes away from his glare. He was sure they were all wondering who the hel he was and what he'd done to win Val's heart where they couldn't. But he didn't care. All he cared about was the fact that she was his, and when he did finally ask her to be his bride, she would say yes.

CHAPTER FOURTEEN

Loki didn't want Val having to walk through the cobblestone streets in heels, so he magicked them to Valhalla's Throne. They landed outside the front door, and Val blinked several times, adjusting to the bright lights and the noise from the crowd waiting to enter.

Her stomach flopped, and she gulped. "I think I'll fly next time."

He looked at her. "You didn't like it?"

She shook her head as her stomach churned again.

"Weird. It's never bothered me. Not much does, though."

"Not even turning into a female horse and giving birth?"

His face grew serious. "Yes, that did, actually. Very much."

She couldn't help but snort. She bent over and sucked in several deep breaths.

Loki rubbed the small of her back. "Are you sure you're all right, love? Maybe I should take you home and pamper you instead of making you sit through dinner."

Val straightened and breathed in. "Nice try, but getting me in your bed isn't in the cards for tonight. Elle is going to be here with your whole family, therefore we are going to be here with your entire family."

Loki nodded and took her hand, leading her to the front door. "So my bed isn't in the cards tonight, but what about your bed? Or my couch? I have a really soft rug in the living room. And then there's the shower, the sunken tub, the-"

She pulled on his tie and brought his lips an inch from hers. "Shut up, or all of those places will be off the cards for the foreseeable future."

He smiled. "Yes, darling."

"And don't call me that while we're in there. I don't want to have to explain anything to anyone. I want to try and get through this night without bloodshed."

His eyes twinkled, and she got the distinct impression he wasn't about to listen to a thing she said.

"You're impossible."

He kissed her nose. "And you're irritating as hel, so we're even."

No. Not in the slightest.

They stepped up to the bouncer, and he looked between Loki and Val, nodded, and let them in.

The inside of Valhalla's Throne kicked Val in the gut. It was like being at an inn back on Asgard- except for the half-naked women, of course.

Valhalla's Throne was so similar to the Helheim side of the Raven Weaver, but more masculine. Deep leather chairs. Dark smoky wood. Rustic red brick walls. Metal ceilings with beams exposed. Dim lighting made everything more mysterious and sensual. It surprised her how much alike Frigg's place and Odin's place were. Maybe it was because they both missed Asgard.

All around, beings played darts and cards. Females of varying races and species wearing small, poofy skirts and little more than a bra delivered drinks and food. The women smiled and laughed with the men, touching them, rubbing their shoulders, ruffling their hair. Yuck.

Several of the women sported heavy wings folded neatly on their backs. A couple more had long pointy tails poking out underneath their skirts. More than half the women sported horns of various sizes and colors.

"See anything you like?" Loki teased.

She elbowed him in the ribs. "Trust me, if I had been so inclined to be with a female, I would definitely have chosen a Valkyrie over this lot any day."

Loki nodded in appreciation.

"Loki?"

Val turned as a bushy mountain man strode toward them with dark hair shaved on the sides and braided on top and down his back, and tattoos covering most of his exposed skin.

Baldur.

Val stiffened, knowing the history between Baldur and Loki, but Baldur simply nodded.

Loki offered his hand, but Baldur looked at it and then folded his arms.

Wow. Talk about someone who couldn't get over the past.

Loki dropped his hand unfazed. "Good to see you back on your feet."

Baldur growled, and Loki chuckled.

"Baldur and I go into the ring every few weeks. He keeps trying to beat me for slights in the past."

"Slights?" said Baldur. "You killed me."

Loki shrugged. "Technically, that was Hödr. I only supplied the arrow."

Baldur grumbled. "Why do you come here? No one wants you."

"Odin wants him," Val said. "He invited Loki and me."

Baldur looked at her for the first time. "That surprises me. Odin doesn't usually allow Loki to bring his one-night stands to family dinners."

"Maybe that's because I'm not a one-night stand," Val spat.

Baldur snorted. "I'm sure they all think that."

Loki's eyes flashed, and he stepped up to Baldur, though he stood a good six inches shorter. "That's enough. I won't tolerate you disrespecting her. Say what you want about me, but never, ever, talk to her that way again. This is Valkyrie. The last remaining of the Valkyrie of old. Show her respect, or I won't wait for the arena to hand you your ass."

Baldur's eyes widened, and he looked at Val. "I apologize."

"Don't say it if you don't mean it," said Val. "Or I'll kick your ass myself."

Loki slipped his arm around her waist before kissing her hair. "Come on, love."

Baldur's eyes almost bugged out of his head.

Val threw Baldur a tight smile. "Nice to see you again, Baldur. I look forward to meeting you in the arena myself sometime."

Baldur didn't reply as she and Loki turned from him and

headed down a hallway to the end. They hit a door, and Loki stopped.

"Maybe this wasn't a good idea." His eyes held uncertainty she'd never witnessed in him before.

Val rolled her eyes. "Are you kidding me? Don't get all insecure now. I dressed up and everything. Plus, if that's the kind of intro I'm gonna get with your family, this dinner is going to be much more interesting than anticipated. I'm not turning back now. Besides," She kissed him. "I don't care what any of them say about you; it won't change a thing. Hel knows I've heard a thousand times worse. I'll stick up for you, don't worry."

Loki shook his head. "Only you would relish putting Norse gods in their place."

She shrugged. "What can I say? I'm a man-eater."

Loki's eyes twinkled. "And what a good little man-eater you are, too."

Val laughed. "You're awful."

He tilted her chin and kissed her. "But you love it."

Loki guided Val through the opulent burlesque chambers to the secluded enclave at the back of the club, where Odin's exclusive sanctuary awaited. They reached the door, and Loki paused before knocking. As they stood before the entrance to Odin's private quarters, a wave of tumultuous emotions surged within Loki.

The echoes of Baldur's cutting words to Val reverberated

in Loki's mind, piercing him with a searing intensity. Despite enduring countless insults over eons, the affront delivered to Val ignited a fiery rage within him, unlike anything before. The thought of Val being insulted fueled a primal urge within Loki, compelling him to unleash his wrath upon Baldur. Making him want to rip out Baldur's tongue and nail it to the wall. Now staring at the door to Odin's home, he wasn't sure he'd be able to hold back again if anyone else said anything to upset or belittle her.

Val had taken Baldur's vocal jab with the same ease she used to deflect physical blows in the arena. And had prompted Loki to regard her with a mixture of awe and pride. How could someone as exquisite and resolute as Val have chosen him? The weight of his unworthiness bore down on Loki, as he grappled with the realization that he was undeserving of her love. Yet, against all odds, she was his, a beacon of light in his dark existence. The mere prospect of losing her threatened to consume him, plunging him into an abyss of despair.

"Are you sure you want to do this?" she finally asked.

With a fleeting smile to mask his inner turmoil, Loki rapped on the door, determined to face whatever lay beyond rather than risk losing Val, the embodiment of beauty and perfection bestowed upon him by the Fates themselves. Because losing her might really be the death of him.

He waited, almost losing his nerve, and deciding to lock her away in his house on the hill forever.

A moment passed, and the door opened.

A tall, broad-shouldered man with a feral air nodded to Loki. "Father."

"Fenrir. How are you this evening, son?"

Fenrir looked between Loki and Val and simply nodded. He sniffed the air and turned his deep-set, ash-colored gaze on her. His heavy brow, thick sideburns, and facial hair belied his werewolf nature. His hair was long and wavy like Loki's, but his tanned skin showed how much more time he'd spent in the sun.

"So, this is her," Fenrir said without pretense.

"Fenrir, this is Valkyrie."

He stared at her for a moment longer and then offered his hand.

Val shook it. "It's nice to meet you, Fenrir."

He snorted. "I doubt that, but thank you for saying it."

Loki frowned. Something had happened. Fenrir was in an even more sullen mood than usual. Guilt struck him. It'd been too long since he'd spent time with his son. He'd been a horrible father before, but in the past hundred years or so, Loki had begun trying a bit more. But in Val's presence, he was acutely aware he hadn't tried enough.

Loki pulled Fenrir into a hug. "Let's talk tomorrow."

Fenrir nodded and removed a piece of paper from his pocket. "I got through the list. They all agreed."

Loki took the paper. "Thank you for doing it. I appreciate it."

Fenrir stepped out of the way, and Loki and Val entered.

"What is that paper?" Val asked.

Loki looked at her. "Alamax's siblings. Fenrir paid them all a visit for us. They agreed not to say anything."

Her eyes narrowed. "How did you get them to agree?"

Loki smiled. "Fenrir can be most charming when he wants."

Val snorted. "You're a terrible liar."

Loki dropped his jaw in mock offense. "How dare you! I invented lying."

Val shook her head, and Loki kissed her hair.

"Don't look a gift horse in the mouth."

Confusion played over Val's features. "What the hel does that even mean?"

"It means you and Elle are safe. So relax and enjoy tonight."

RELIEF FLOODED VAL. SHE WANTED TO BELIEVE LOKI, BUT still wasn't convinced. She'd had one fallen angel lie to her that week. What was to say the others wouldn't lie as well? She would have to question Loki more about it later; now wasn't the time.

The space opened up like a private house tucked behind the world. Exposed timber beams ran the length of the ceiling, their light grain polished to a muted honey sheen. The cream-colored walls held various abstract paintings. The floors were a creamy stone, and a thick white rug anchored the center of the room with a huge glass coffee table filled with water where two beautiful koi fish swam back and forth.

As Fenrir closed the door, the sounds of the club shut out, cocooning them in their own little world. An ample leather sectional hosted half a dozen people. Large soft-looking pillows in golds and silvers adorned every few feet of the couch, along with a shimmery plush blanket.

Behind the sectional, a wall of French doors stood open, leading to a yard. Odin tended to a deep fire pit, cooking meat and drinking from a mug while talking to two men. Lush grass, flowering shrubs, and even several blossoming trees rustled in a slight breeze. Two ravens circled above Odin's head, swooping at the meat. And two large wolves lounged on the grass, tails swishing as they watched the invaders of their territory.

"Val," Frigg called from a metal bar in the corner. She waved and walked over.

"Hello, Lady Frigg," said Val.

Frigg chuckled. "Just Frigg, and I'm so glad the shoes fit. I was pretty sure they would. They go perfectly with that dress, too."

Loki looked down. "Did I not get you shoes?"

Val shook her head. "I figured sneakers or boots weren't the best match. Somehow Frigg knew too, so she sent me these."

Frigg waved her off. "It was nothing, dear. I'm glad you came." She produced two drinks and set them on the counter. "You too, Loki. It's been too long since the whole family was together."

Loki nodded. "Agreed. And I commend you for getting Fenrir to come. Only Hel is missing, but then she rarely joins us."

Frigg nodded. "She's always invited, but she's also quite busy."

Val and Loki sat at the bar, and there was a knock on the door. Fenrir opened the door for Thor and Elle, and Val stiffened and scanned the room for danger as she always did.

Frigg patted Val's hand and headed out from behind the bar.

Loki sipped his drink. "You're perfectly safe here."

She cocked an eyebrow at him. "Are you?"

He shrugged.

"Exactly." Frigg hugged and welcomed Elle and Thor.

Val turned to her drink and sniffed the liquid. "What is this?"

Loki smiled and winked at Val. "Mana of the gods."

She eyed him skeptically and sipped it. Her taste buds exploded. Every favorite flavor she'd ever tasted rolled across her tongue and blended together.

She swallowed hard and stared at the glass. "What the hel was that?"

"Like I said, mana of the gods. What did it taste like?"

"What do you mean? You tasted it."

"It tastes different for everyone." He sipped his glass again.

Val picked up his glass and sniffed it, and then sniffed her own. They smelled the same.

"Mine tastes like chocolate dripped over strawberries with a hint of cinnamon toast at the end," said Loki.

"Mine is butterscotch-covered ice cream with notes of Irish crème, nutmeg, and peanut butter cookies, I guess. There are other flavors as well, but too many to catch them all."

Loki nodded and sipped his again. "And over the years, the taste will change depending on your favorites as well."

Val stared at her glass and then took another sip. It was the coolest thing she'd ever ingested.

"Thor!" The man who'd been talking to Odin hugged Thor.

He hugged Elle, and then Hödr walked over to greet her as well.

“Does Hödr blame you for what happened with Baldur?”

Loki shrugged. “If he does, he’s not let on. Hödr’s… different. He’s not like the others. He takes everything in stride, and he doesn’t hold on to the past. He’s honestly the only sane one of us.”

Val laughed. She’d never met Hödr before. He’d been killed by Váli before she’d been born, but she’d heard the stories. It amazed her that with all the gods had gone through, they were still relatively civil to one another.

“So who is that?” she pointed to the man who had hugged Elle.

“Meili, Thor’s brother.” Loki pointed to the couch. “That’s Váli. And next to him with the longer blond hair is Vidarr. You know Tyr and Hermódr.”

She nodded. She’d fought alongside both of them in battle before. Tyr, the god of war, Hermódr, his best friend and messenger of the gods, and Vidarr, god of vengeance- also known for being the god of silence as well. Where Tyr and Vid were the strongest beings Val had ever seen in battle, Herm was the fastest by far. Faster than even Alamax. For a moment, she wondered if Herm fought Alamax, if either one would actually get a hit in, or if they’d just fly around each other until they both exhausted themselves.

"Chow's ready," Odin called.

Loki finished his drink and led Val out to the atrium. The giant room with a tall ceiling that went straight up into what looked like the actual sky, but it could have been an exceedingly intricate painting. White fabric and glowing light bulbs had been strung from beam to beam, creating an intimate, romantic effect. In the center of the room stood an enormous rustic wood table.

Odin carried a massive platter of meat to the table and set it in the middle. When he looked up at her, she saw that only one small bruise remained from their encounter.

He smiled at her. "Valkyrie. Welcome. Thank you for joining us."

His words were a punch to the gut. What was she supposed to say? He'd smiled at her, welcomed her, and not called her daughter.

"Thank you for inviting me." The words fell from her lips mechanically, and she couldn't believe she'd said them.

Odin bowed and then walked back to the fire pit.

"Wow," Loki whispered. "That showed amazing restraint. I had no idea you could do that."

She glared at him, and he snickered.

She sat in the seat in front of her and watched Odin as the others took their seats.

After a moment of chatting with Hermódr, Loki took his seat next to her and slipped his hand between her thighs, making her body heat.

Thor pulled out a seat for Elle next to Val, and Val brushed Loki's hand away. He growled and put his hand right back in the same place.

So irritating.

CHAPTER FIFTEEN

Loki sat through the meal, allowing his hand to drift ever so subtly up Val's thigh. The higher his fingers reached, the warmer her skin grew, and the more flustered she became.

More than once, she'd shoved his hand away, but he'd smiled and put it right back where he wanted it. Teasing her was more fun than he'd anticipated. However, when Fenrir sniffed the air and looked up at them, Loki finally stopped. Having a bit of fun under the table was one thing. Others at the table, knowing what was happening, was something quite different.

Fenrir shook his head and went back to his dinner. Loki's heart went out to him. As far as he knew, Fenrir had never had a woman of his own. His feral and unpredictable nature kept him from getting too close to anyone. Partly out of fear of being hurt, and partly out of fear of hurting someone else.

Loki's vision clouded, and flickers of the future flashed in and out of view. Fenrir at Frigg's masquerade. A woman. A fight and then… nothing.

Loki's fork clattered to his plate, and he sucked in a breath.

"Are you all right?" asked Val.

Loki nodded and grabbed his ale, chugging the entire thing.

"Father?"

Loki stared at Fenrir, unable to voice what he'd seen. It'd been a while since he'd gotten flashes. The sensation confused and made him anxious at the same time.

"Loki, can I get you another drink?" Frigg's soft voice floated down the table. His gaze connected with hers, and she gave him a tight, knowing smile. "Come on," she said. "Let's get you something stronger."

Mutely, Loki nodded and stood, not bothering to look at Val's questioning stare or meet Fenrir's eye.

He walked to the bar and leaned on it. Frigg pulled out a bottle of mana and poured him a wide glass.

Loki chugged it without actually tasting it.

"Future flashes?" she asked.

Loki nodded and pointed at the glass. Frigg poured him half a glass, and he downed it. She corked the bottle and put it away.

"Any more of that and we will be carrying you out of here," she said.

"I can handle my mana."

She nodded. "Of course you can. All of you men can. Until you can't."

Elle and Meili passed them and headed to the kitchen sink to wash dishes.

Loki stared at Frigg for a long minute before she squeezed his hand.

"Do you want to talk about it?"

He shook his head. "Not tonight. But… did you see it?"

She looked over at Fenrir. "I've seen… something."

"A woman."

She nodded. "It may not be bad."

"And then again, it might be." He shook his head. "Fenrir has been through enough in his life. Doesn't he deserve happiness too? Me for a father… or lack of one. Odin's punishment. Tyr's betrayal. It's left him broken and alone."

Frigg smiled. "I always knew you were a softy on the inside."

Loki barked with laughter. "Oh, really?"

Frigg shrugged. "You forget I've known you longer than anyone else. Even as a child, I saw who you were supposed to be. I know you, Loki of the *Jötunn*. And I love you all the same."

Though the relationships between the older gods like him, Odin, Frigg, Heimdall, and Tyr were a bit hazy, they'd all been around almost since the beginning. And Loki and Frigg had been closer than most when they'd been younger. And despite everything, she'd always loved him like a sister. Even after what he'd done to Baldur. He didn't know how she did it. How she'd put up with them all for so many centuries. Her and Freya. Even Hel hadn't put up with them and had taken residence somewhere else. But not Frigg. She stayed with them. Cared for them. Fought for them and their happiness without ever asking anything in return for herself.

Loki squeezed her hand. "Next week we will talk."

She nodded. “I’m always here.” She had the gentlest, most nurturing nature of any being he’d ever met, and the day she received her own fated mate, he would cheer alongside all of the rest of them and protect her until the end.

Lightning hit the floor near the table, and Hödr flew out of his chair.

"Thor!" Odin yelled. "Enough."

Val jumped from her seat and rushed to Elle. Twin silver and golden blades protruded from her wrist bracelets.

Thor looked like he might strike Val next, and Loki appeared next to her instantly- blue magic skimming his hands.

Thor’s breath came out heavy as lightning flecked his eyes. He scanned the room where half the table had gotten up and moved away, and the other half remained in their seats, silent.

"Did all of you know?" Thor yelled. "Am I the only one not in on the joke?"

Thunder rolled louder above the building.

So he’d finally found out the truth.

"Thor." Frigg moved gracefully toward him. "It's not like that. Elle's mother was a dear friend who Surtr kidnapped at Ragnarök. We thought she had died. When Val sent me word about Elle, I had to help. I loved her mother like a sister. And Val is a Valkyrie. One of our own."

Thor looked to her. "You. You're the one who told me to come to your masquerade. You knew she would be there. You knew we would meet."

Frigg didn’t even stiffen at the accusation. "Your fate and the fate of the fire giants have been tied together since the beginning of time. Did I know it would be Surtr's daughter who would heal your heart? No. I only knew someone would. And that someone would be from the house of Surtr."

Val took a step toward, but Loki put his hand on Val's arm to stop her from getting any closer. "He won't hurt her."

"And you." Thor looked to Odin. "You knew who she was when you saw us together, didn't you?"

Odin crossed his sinewy arms over his chest. "Yes."

Thor grabbed his hammer from inside his jacket and pointed it skyward before anyone spoke. His feet lifted from the floor, and he took off into the sky.

Elle set down the dish towel she'd been using and walked toward the exit.

Val grasped her arm and turned her around. Elle stared at her for a moment.

"I should have told him," she said.

Val's mouth opened and closed several times.

Elle peered around the group and offered a weak smile. "Thank you all for a lovely meal. I think I should go."

"Elle, stay," said Frigg. "Thor will move beyond this. Trust me."

Elle nodded. "Thank you, Lady Frigg, but I think I'd like to go back to my apartment."

"I'll take you," said Val.

"I don't want you to miss out."

"Let me take you," Meili offered.

Elle shook her head. "I'll be fine."

Frigg walked to her side and linked her arm with Elle's. "I'll go. I have to go pick up a few things at the Raven Weaver anyway."

"Thank you, Lady Frigg."

Frigg laid her hand on Elle's arm. "Frigg. Or Auntie Frigg, if you prefer. I meant what I said. Your mother was like a sister to me."

Elle nodded, and they walked out the door together.

Val sheathed her blades and went to follow them, but Loki grasped her hand.

"Where do you think you're going?" Loki asked.

"To make sure they are okay."

Loki touched her cheek. Always the protector. "Frigg's got her. They'll be fine."

"But-"

"Let her go, Signe. She needs to stand on her own two feet. You can't protect her forever, not from this. She needs to learn how to take care of herself, especially if she is going to be in a relationship with Thor."

Val looked like she might protest, but then her shoulders slumped.

"Would you like to finish your dinner?"

She shook her head. "I'm not hungry. But I feel bad that all this food will go to waste."

Loki snorted. "Obviously, you've never seen Fenrir and Tyr eat. I was afraid there might not be enough when we arrived."

Val smiled up at him. "So, what was the deal at the table? You left so suddenly."

"I just had some future flashes."

"Of us?"

He shook his head. "No. I never have flashes of my own life. These were about Fenrir."

Val looked back at the table where Fenrir continued to chow down as if nothing had happened.

"Is it bad?" she asked.

Loki stared at Fenrir. "I… I'm not sure."

"But the flashes upset you."

Loki tried to figure out how to phrase what he'd seen. "They were… ominous."

Val squeezed his hand. "I'm sorry."

He wrapped his arms around her and pulled her in tight. The dinner had started out so well, and had then gone downhill so rapidly that he'd been caught unprepared. He wasn't sure what to say. He just hoped he got more flashes so he could get some more clarity before talking to Fenrir about what he'd seen.

"I'm sorry that this first dinner turned out to be such a disaster for you."

She snorted. "Really? That was a disaster? I honestly expected so much more from you lot. You've all become almost boring in your old ages."

Loki looked at her. "Old age? Do I look old to you?" He leaned in closer. "Do I feel old to you?"

She smiled. "You do not."

Well, thank the Fates for that at least.

"Do you want to go and fight downstairs?" she asked.

Loki shook his head. "Not in the mood. But we could utilize one of the recovery rooms."

Val sighed. "Not in the mood. But if you want to go catch a burlesque show while I head home, I understand."

She understood? Understood what? "I'd think you should know by now that you are the only woman I want to see naked from here on out."

Val smiled and then kissed him.

"Come on," he said. "Let's return you to your apartment. You won't stop worrying until you see Elle's okay." He raised his hand to snap his fingers, but she stopped him.

"I'd like to walk it," she said.

"Your wish is my command, love."

CHAPTER SIXTEEN

After saying their goodbyes, Val and Loki strolled back to Frigg's place in silence. Val was too worried about Elle to talk, and whatever Loki had glimpsed in the future had him more troubled. He carried her sparkly shoes, allowing her feet to relax for the first time in hours. She'd never worn high heels before, and though she found herself quite adept at wearing them, they weren't at all comfortable. Give her a pair of sneakers or boots any day. Something sturdy and easy to move in.

Val had known Thor would react badly, but she didn't like the way he'd treated Elle. If she'd been there, she would have punched him in the throat for making Elle look so small and desperate. Elle had come so far, and though Val had told her it wouldn't go over well, she wished she had been wrong. She would rather have been wrong than see Elle so hurt.

"She's going to be okay," Loki finally said. "Thor has a hot temper, but he will calm down and see that he loves her and it doesn't matter who her father is."

She crossed her arms over her chest. "How do you know? He hasn't been forgiving in the past."

Loki touched her cheek, sending warmth through her. "Because he has to. He's tried for centuries to move on, and he hasn't been able to, but this is his chance. His last chance. He will realize that. He will figure out that if he doesn't get past this, he will lose her and his one true chance at happiness. And honestly, I've never seen him look at a woman the way he looks at her. In the end, he will forgive her because if he doesn't, he will hate himself even more than he does now."

Loki's words were heartfelt and sound, but from what Val had seen, Thor and a few others hadn't truly given up the past. And if they hadn't moved on after all this time, could they ever? She paused. She was the same. And if she didn't give up holding on to the past, she would end up angry, bitter, and without Loki. The time had come. She needed to move on. Move forward. With Loki.

"Are you okay?" Loki asked.

She looked at him. "I think I am."

Loki held the door to the Raven Weaver for her, and they walked inside. A strange chill fell over her shoulders as they entered, and she shivered.

"Why is it so cold in here?" she asked.

"Hmmm…" Loki touched the wall. "Looks like Frigg forgot to renew her protection wards. Her goodness is what gives this place its warm, peaceful feeling, but when she leaves, the darkness of the patrons seeps into the walls, leaving a chill in the air. So she imbues the place with part of her essence to keep it safe while she is away. She must have forgotten in all that's been going on."

Interesting. Val knew Frigg was powerful, but to actually be able to infuse a place with her goodness was power beyond what she'd seen before.

As if hearing them speak, Frigg appeared from the portal and spotted them. She nodded and then moved behind the bar.

Val blew out a breath. From Frigg's expression, it looked as though Elle was not doing well.

"I need to talk to Heimdall," Loki said.

Val nodded, and together they walked through the portal.

They stopped at the top of the stairs inside the upper bar, when the door opened, and Heimdall walked in from the Midgardian street.

Interesting. Val had never seen him use the door to Midgard before. He'd only ever used the portal down to Helheim. She wondered where Heimdall lived. From how much he lived in the pub, she wouldn't be surprised if he lived in the building somewhere.

He walked straight to them. "He's already done pouting."

Val glanced at the stairs up to the apartments. She took a step toward them, but Heimdall touched her arm.

"Not yet," he said. "We need to see how this plays out."

Plays out? What did he mean by that? The hairs on her arms raised. Something was happening.

Thor rushed down the stairs and looked around wildly.

"Have you seen Elle?" he demanded.

"She's upstairs." Icy chills rushed down Val's spine.

Thor shook his head. "Her apartment looks like there's been a fight."

Dread drenched Val's gut, making her want to throw up. She raced up the stairs to Elle's apartment. Loki followed closely behind.

"Elle!" Val yelled. "Elle, answer me, now!" She burst through the door to Elle's apartment.

The table was overturned, and one of Elle's shoes lay sideways on the floor. Val stormed into the bathroom and caught a scent that made her stomach churn.

No.

She turned to Loki. "You said we were safe."

His eyebrows drew together. "You are. I made sure of it. The hunters all gave their word."

"Then how the hel did Thadren know where Elle was?"

Loki shook his head. "I… I have no idea, but it wasn't any of Alamax's siblings."

Shit. Shit, shit, shit!

"I have to go." Val brushed past him and headed for her apartment.

"Where?" Loki asked.

"Where do you think? Muspelheim to get Elle."

"Well, you aren't going alone." Loki snapped his fingers, and his royal Asgardian armor morphed onto his body like a blue snakeskin suit. A royal robe draped around his shoulders, and a silver helmet with horns that mimicked his real ones protruded from the front.

Val unzipped her dress and let it drop to the floor as she walked to her closet and yanked a trunk from inside.

She laid her hands on it for a moment, and then she threw it open, revealing her golden armor.

Footsteps raced down the hallway, and she turned to the door. Frigg appeared, out of breath.

"Thor is gone. He took Tanngrisnir and Tanngnjóstr and is already headed to Muspelheim," she breathed.

Loki nodded. "Where are the others?"

"With Odin. They are on their way."

"Very good," said Loki. "We will join you presently. I just need to run an errand first."

Frigg disappeared out of the doorway.

Loki set his hand on Val's shoulder. "You dress. I'll be back before you finish."

"Where are you going?"

"To get reinforcements." With a snap of his fingers, Loki disappeared.

"Seriously? He couldn't snap my armor on, too?" She shook her head. They were definitely going to have to have a conversation about how he used his powers from now on.

Loki returned just as Val finished getting her shoulder pauldrons on, and he wasn't alone. With no time for introductions, Loki walked to her and threw his arm around her waist.

"Time to go, love."

Val drew her blade. "I'm ready."

Loki turned to the woman behind him, and she smiled.

"See you there," said the beautiful, gothic-looking woman who greatly resembled Loki.

With a snap of her fingers, she disappeared, and then so did Loki and Val.

Val barely had time to grab onto him before everything dissolved, and her stomach jumped into her tonsils. She squeezed her eyes shut when they landed with a flash and a bump.

Damn, Val hated traveling like that. But she would rather be tortured at Surtr's hands than let any of the gathered group see how queasy it made her.

Val tried to orient herself. They stood in the doorway leading to Surtr's throne room. In the front stood two enormous goats, protecting Elle and Thor from Surtr and Thadren.

Surtr and Thadren's men stood on either side of the hall, waiting for a battle.

"I see your ego hasn't diminished over time," said Odin.

"His undeserved ego," Loki added.

Surtr turned his eyes on the group, and Loki took half a step in front of her.

"My ego is nothing compared to yours, Loki, son of a *Jötunn*. You should be siding with your own kind. Are you here to stab Asgardians in the back again and help me instead?"

Loki pulled his blades from the air, his clothing changed from Asgardian to *Jötunn*, his frame grew to his true height, and he pulled off his helmet, revealing his own horns.

Loki took a step forward, but Val stuck out her arm to stop him. He turned his diamond-colored eyes on her.

She shook her head. "Not your fight."

Loki looked as if weighing her words.

"Come on, Asgardians," Surtr taunted. "I will take you all on at once. And then I'll go to what is left of Asgard and obliterate the rest of your rainbow bridge. And there is nothing any of you can do about it."

Odin flung his spear at Surtr, but Surtr caught it and flung it back. Odin grabbed Frigg around the waist and hoisted her sideways before she was impaled. Thor's brothers swore and pushed forward, protecting Frigg like a football team.

"Try hurting my mother again, and I'll rip this entire structure down with you still inside," yelled Baldur.

Loki disappeared and reappeared behind Surtr. He drove both blades into Surtr's back, but they melted, and the hilts clattered to the ground at Loki's feet.

"Was that meant to hurt?" Surtr swung around and struck Loki, knocking him across the room.

Hel no! Val released her wings and took to the air, grabbing Loki and spiraling sideways. She wrapped her wings around him, and they tumbled across a table, making Surtr's men back up.

They landed with Loki on top of her, and he smiled. "I thought you said you weren't in the mood tonight."

Val rolled her eyes. "I just saved your life, you idiot."

He raised a dark blue eyebrow. "You do realize I'm half frost giant, right? A little toss across the room won't hurt me."

"But landing in that giant fireplace will."

Loki followed her gaze and nodded. "True."

Fenrir roared and raced forward. Hermódr went to grab Fen but missed, and Fenrir got several yards closer.

Loki jumped from the table, but Val grabbed his arm.

"Fenrir, no!" Loki shouted.

"Brother!" came a sharp voice from the back of the group.

Fenrir stopped. "I can take him," he roared.

"Sorry, I'm afraid not. But I can." Hel stepped out of the

group from where she'd arrived with Val and Loki minutes before.

"You... you can't be here." Surtr's voice shook. "You aren't allowed."

Hel shrugged, making her ebony hair shimmer in the firelight. "I spoke to my boss and got special permission to leave my realm. I've never seen him excited about the prospect of someone coming into his realm. He's never met a fire giant before. And you… Well, your reputation precedes you. You've eluded me for too long, Surtr. Your reign is over."

For the first time, fear crossed Surtr's heavy features.

"Go with her," said Thor. "Or we will make you go."

Surtr licked his lips. "Thadren, ready your men."

Thadren looked at Elle and then Thor's family.

"Wait," Elle blurted.

All eyes turned to her. She looked straight at Thadren. "As heir to the throne, I will give you Muspelheim, all of it, if you do nothing."

"You have no right to offer that," said Surtr.

"I do. When you leave for Helheim, I will be in charge. And as your successor, I have the right to abdicate the throne and to give it to whomever I deem the strongest and best to lead your people. And I choose Thadren."

Thadren looked as if he were calculating his options. "You do not want the throne?"

"No," said Elle.

He studied her for a moment and then looked at Thor. "You choose him?"

She nodded.

Thadren's expression fell for a fraction of a moment. He

said something Val couldn't hear and then ran a gentle finger down her cheek before pulling his hand away. His expression hardened, and he looked at Surtr. "We will not fight."

Surtr bellowed a guttural roar that reverberated through the cavernous hall. His fiery eyes blazed with unrelenting fury. With a deafening crash, he launched himself at Thadren, the massive blade in his hand gleaming like liquid fire. The ground quaked beneath his weight as he closed the distance in two thunderous strides.

"Thadren! No!" Elle's voice rang out, hands trembling as she summoned her magic. Her chest heaved with exertion, her fingers tingling with raw energy that begged to be unleashed. Her power coursed through her veins, hot and wild. She raised her hands and thrust them forward, releasing a crackling surge of violent energy that illuminated the hall in an otherworldly glow.

“Damn,” said Loki. “Why were you protecting her all this time? Looks like she can take care of herself.

“Because she can't control her powers. She hasn't learned how yet. Trust me, I have more than one scar to prove it, and so do the walls of her old bedroom.”

Elle pulled her arms back, then threw them forward. Ropes wrapped around Surtr's torso, pinning his arms down and dropping him to the floor.

Surtr roared as he struggled against the magical bindings. His movements violent but futile. Each attempt to break free only tightened the ropes further. He stumbled under their weight before collapsing onto the cold floor with a crash.

“You were saying?” Loki cocked an eyebrow at her.

Val gaped in surprise.

"You think this will hold me forever?" he sneered.

"They may not burn you, but they cannot be broken."

"Let me out of these, or I'll kill you," Surtr yelled.

Elle closed her hand and turned her wrist. The ropes tightened against Surtr, and he struggled to breathe.

Without warning, one of the giant goats reared back and head-butted Surtr, sending him flying into the stone wall. Surtr crumpled, and the other goat kicked him in the stomach.

“Wow,” said Val. “You don’t happen to have two giant goats, do you?”

Loki smiled. “I don’t need goats. I’m my own giant.”

Surtr groaned and rolled on his back. "I'll eat both of you and break all your bones, so you can't come back," he roared at the goats.

Hel pushed the goats aside with ease.

"All right, you giant walking sweaters, I can handle things from here." She stopped over Surtr and lowered her trident to his chest.

He flexed against the ropes, and one of them snapped. "I will kill you, daughter."

Hel pressed her trident into his chest as another rope snapped.

Surtr yelled out, and Elle threw more fiery ropes at him. The new ropes sprouted clawed hooks at the ends and bit into Surtr's skin.

"Don't worry," said Hel. "I got this." She turned to Surtr. "Surtr, king of the fire giants. Murderer of Asgardians. I, Hel, daughter of Loki and Goddess of Death, do hereby commit you to the depths of Helheim, as a prisoner. Never again to hurt anyone."

Before Surtr protested, Hel pressed the trident into his chest. It passed through him and hit the floor below. Surtr screamed in agony as the black smoke encircled him. It started at his chest and swirled outward until he was cocooned. Elle's ropes disappeared under their inky depths.

A giant black pit opened in the floor, and he dropped through.

The stones of the floor rolled back into place, and the black smoke sucked back into Hel's trident and snaked up her arm and disappeared into her dress.

"Remind me to never piss off your daughter," said Val.

Loki chuckled. "Nah. I think you could take her."

Val shook her head. Was he delusional?

Hel turned to Thor. "I believe that concludes my reason for being here, yes?"

Thor nodded. "Thank you, cousin."

Hel smiled. "No. Thank you. I haven't had this much fun since... forever. And now I go to make sure Surtr is completely uncomfortable in his new abode." She winked at Elle. "Be sure to come visit me when you have time. I'd love to pick your brain about the best ways to torture him." Hel backed through a shadowy portal and disappeared before Elle answered.

No one moved for several seconds as they stared at the spot where Surtr had lain. Then Thor rushed to Elle.

Baldur pushed to the front of the group and looked around. "Is that it?"

"No fighting?" Vidarr moaned.

"Man, I got all dressed up and have nowhere to go," said Hermódr. "This armor isn't easy to get on."

"Perhaps the new fire giant king will allow us to spar with some of his men, so it isn't a total waste," said Hödr.

The group looked at Thadren.

"Of course," Thadren offered. "Anything we can do to heal relations with the Asgardians."

"Can we kill them?" Fenrir growled.

"No!" everyone said together.

"You lot really have gone soft." Fenrir stalked to the door and ran out.

Loki looked at Val and smiled. "Shall we?"

"After you."

"No, my love, after you. You show me which ones hurt you in your time here, and I will make sure they suffer."

Val couldn't help the smile that spread across her face. "The more you make them suffer, the more I'll give you to enjoy when we get home."

Loki produced his blades and grinned. "Then they will suffer unimaginably."

EPILOGUE

Three Months Later

Val stared at the white stick and blinked.

Still the same.

She closed her eyes again. Please. Please, Fates, do not let this happen.

She opened her eyes again. The stick remained the same.

Val's heart beat like a war drum. It was too soon. She wasn't ready. Loki wasn't ready.

She looked at the stick again, as if by some miracle, simply staring at it, the little lines would disappear. A soft knock sounded on the door.

"You all right, love?"

Val swallowed hard. "Yup. I'm good." She flushed the toilet, shoved the stick into her pocket, then washed her hands and opened the door.

"You still sick?" He felt her forehead.

Val shook her head.

"You sure? You feel kind of clammy."

She swatted his hand away. "I said I'm fine." She stomped to their bed and crawled back under the covers as her stomach gurgled.

A minute passed, and then the bed dipped down as Loki curled up behind her and wrapped an arm around her.

"Signe, what did I do to irritate you now? Tell me, and I'll apologize."

Val snorted. Right. How did you apologize for getting someone pregnant?

She blew out a breath. Pregnant. She was pregnant. "It's nothing. I'm fine."

"Why do you bother lying to me? You know I can tell."

"Because one of these days I am hoping you will take the hint and leave me alone."

His body stiffened, and his arm slid from around her.

"Sorry," she mumbled. "I'm just… tired."

Loki kissed her head. "I have some meetings, but I'll be back in a while. Are you going to go to the Raven Weaver today?"

She shook her head. Ever since she'd started living with Loki, she'd spent less and less time working at the bar and more and more time redecorating the house.

Loki had told her to do whatever she wanted with the place, so she had. And to her surprise, she'd found she was quite good at it. She had a flair for patterns, textiles, and colors. In the past months, their house had gone from stark white modern to a warm, posh, inviting environment. Even Loki had remarked on how much he enjoyed the new atmosphere.

"What time will you be back?" she asked.

Loki smiled. "I'll bring lunch."

She looked over at him. "Can you bring Chinese?"

"Of course." He headed for the bedroom door.

"And some garlic bread from Santo's?"

He smiled. "Sure."

"And some carrot cake from Butter Bakery?"

Loki looked back at her. "Are you sure you feel up to eating all that? You haven't been able to keep much down for a week."

She shrugged. "I'll pace myself."

He chuckled. "It's your funeral. See you in a bit. Love you." He took a step but stopped and turned back. He made a swooshing movement with his hand, and a vase filled with dozens of red roses appeared on her nightstand.

"What are those for?"

"To apologize for whatever I've done that has upset you so much."

She sighed. "I'm not mad at you."

He nodded. "If you say so." He walked down the hallway as Val lay in bed, waiting for what would come next.

Every day since she'd moved in, he'd gone through the same routine. He'd gotten up. Showered. Dressed. Gotten ready for work and stopped at the outer door to ask her the same question.

"Are you going to marry me today?" he called.

There it was. Val closed her eyes and bit her tongue to keep from saying yes. A baby. They were going to have a baby.

"Not today," she replied.

Loki laughed. "Love you, future wife."

And then he was gone.

Val lay in bed for a long time, staring at the wall. What the hell did she know about having babies? She'd never even held one until Elle had been born. And sure, she'd raised Elle, but that had been different. She'd been Elle's guardian. Her protector. Her friend. Not her mother.

"Mother." Val said the word out loud, letting it ring in the air. "Mother."

She touched her belly. She was going to be a mother.

Loki sat across from Val, watching her pick at her food. He'd brought her everything she'd asked for, and still, she ate barely anything. It wasn't like her at all. One of the things he loved about her was her healthy appetite for everything in life, like him.

"Do you not like it?" he asked.

She put her fork in the carton of noodles and pushed it away. "It's good. Thank you."

The niggling feeling that had been growing inside Loki for days started to make his skin itch, as if tiny wires had been attached to his hair. Was she tired of him already?

"Do you want the carrot cake?" he asked.

She shook her head and sipped her water.

"Is there something else I can get you?"

She gave him a weak smile. "No. Thank you."

Loki set down his fork, trying not to explode from nervousness. "All right, spit it out."

She looked up at him, confused.

"Are you tired of me? Do you not like the house? Do you want to go back to working at Frigg's full-time? What is it?"

Her silence was a punch to the gut. Her eyes misted, and she blinked several times.

His gut plummeted. Holy crap. She was crying. She never cried. "So, it's me then."

"No. Well, yes, it has to do with you, but no, it's not you."

He tried not to panic, but worry clawed up his throat. "Are you done with me? Don't love me anymore? Don't trust me? Did I not manscape enough?"

"Loki, it isn't any of that. I do love you. And you manscape enough for the both of us, it's just-"

"Just what?" He held his breath waiting. If she left him, he'd not be able to exist anymore. He might as well go live with Hel. Even her daily tortures would be nothing in comparison to what he'd feel daily in his soul without Signe. She'd shown him what life could be like to be his true self, and he could never go back. Neither could he go forward without her support.

Val pulled something from her back pocket and pushed it across the glass table.

Loki looked at it and blinked twice. "A thermometer?"

Val blew out a harsh breath and crossed her arms over her chest. "No, dummy. Why would I give you a thermometer? Turn it over. "

He picked up the white stick and turned it over. He stared at it. A plus sign?

He looked at her. "Okay."

She buried her face in her hands. "I'm pregnant."

Loki stared at the white stick. Tiny writing on the side read: 'Plus means pregnant, minus means not pregnant'.

Pregnant. Signe was pregnant.

Fire bloomed in Loki's chest. He couldn't believe it. A baby. They were going to have a baby.

Loki dropped the stick and rushed around the table, grabbing Val, hugging her tight, and kissing her hair.

"Parents. We're going to be parents." He cupped her face. "Signe, thank you. Thank you. Thank you."

"What? Why are you thanking me? I didn't do this… well, I mean, I did do this, but you did it too. Thank yourself."

He searched her face. "You aren't happy."

"Happy? No, I'm not happy. I'm freaking terrified! I don't have room to be happy."

"But why? Did you not want kids?"

"I don't know. I never gave it much thought. What if I'm a terrible mother? Hel knows you weren't the best father. What if the baby is a werewolf like Fenrir? Or the god of despair or something? Or what if-"

"What if it looks like me, a *Jötunn*?"

"What? No. That's stupid. Our child would be lucky to look like you. Don't be daft."

Loki smiled and kissed her. "And I would be happy to have a child with you who was any of those things. Whether our child has wings, or horns, or is the goddess of malaise, I do not care because it will be our child. And we will all be together."

Her gaze softened, and she hugged him tight.

"You know what this means now, don't you?"

"No."

He broke into a grin. "It means you have to marry me now."

Val pushed away from him. "No, it doesn't."

Loki smiled. "It does. You have to marry me."

"No."

"Yes."

"No," she insisted.

He smiled bigger. "Today."

"Are you crazy?"

Loki got down on one knee and pulled a box from the air.

"Stop," Val demanded.

"Signe, will you marry me?"

"No."

Loki took the ring out of the box and slipped it on her finger.

"Do you want Odin to marry us, or Lucifer?"

Val looked at the ring and then back at him. "I am not deciding that today."

Loki nodded. "Odin then."

"Stop it!"

"I can get word to everyone and have them at Odin's place within the hour. You can wear the dress I bought you. I bet Elle would love to come over and help you with your hair."

"I still haven't said yes."

Loki looked at Val and touched her cheek. "The first time you kissed me, you said yes. The first time you encouraged me to show you my true form, you said yes. When you risked your life to save mine from the fireplace on Muspelheim, you said yes. And every time we make love, you say yes... A lot actually."

Val opened her mouth but then closed it again. “Why do you do that?”

“What?”

“Get all beautifully poetic and stuff?”

He kissed her hand. “Because I say yes.”

She smiled.

“Signe. Will you marry me today?”

She touched his cheek. “Yes.”

THE END

FENRIR'S INNOCENT MATE

GODS AND MONSTERS FATED MATES

Rebekah R. Ganiere

CHAPTER ONE

Grace held her mother's hand and bowed her head to their joined fingers, kissing them. Her mother squeezed her hand tight and took a ragged breath. Grace raised her tear-stung eyes and fought to be strong.

The scent of death filled the bedroom stronger than it had in the past two months, and Grace knew Fay's time drew near. What she didn't understand was why. Why was her mother sick? Why was her life being cut short by disease? She couldn't put the pieces together to figure it out. Shifters didn't get sick. Not even a cold. So getting cancer was unheard of. Grace wondered if it had been because Fay's mate had left when she'd adopted Grace as her own, but no one spoke of what had happened between Fay and her mate. So she didn't think that was it. Besides, that had been over twenty years ago.

Fay took a wheezy breath and smiled at Grace. "It's time, my Goddess child. Call them in."

Grace fought to hold back more tears. She didn't know

what her mother wanted to tell the elders. But they would follow her mother's wishes, whatever they were. When Fay's mate, Grace's biological father, the Alpha of their pack, had disappeared, Fay took charge. Being an Alpha herself, she had held the pack together. Under her rule, the Midnight Moon Pack had thrived.

Even though everyone knew Fay wasn't Grace's biological mother, they had accepted Grace without question. They'd treated Grace with both love and respect. She'd always thought it was because Grace was the former Alpha's daughter, but then Fay had told her the truth of her birth. Grace's mother hadn't just been another shifter female that her father had cheated with. It had been the Moon Goddess Luna herself. Unable to bear her children, Fay had happily accepted the gift of Grace from the Goddess. It had been Fay's mate, Grace's father, who hadn't been able to deal with the results of his infidelity.

"Grace, your destiny lies far from these woods," Fay had said. "You must go before it's too late."

Grace shook her head. "I won't leave you."

Fay brushed the hair from Grace's face. "My sweet Goddess child. You have been the light of my life, but you and I both know this is not where you belong. You cannot remain here after I'm gone. Your light and power are reserved for someone of far nobler birth than any of the males here. Not to mention that you aren't like the rest of us. You are different. You know what I speak of."

Grace did know. It was the reason she'd never shifted in front of anyone but her mom. Why she never ran with the pack. Why she never partook in the mating rituals. She was no normal shifter.

"Promise me. Promise you will go far away and find the person you were meant for."

Fay squeezed Grace's hand so tight she was afraid it would break. It surprised Grace how much strength her mother had left in that moment. It had been a week since she'd been able to hold utensils to feed herself.

"But… where will I find someone like that?"

"The Underworld. Go to the Underworld. Someone there is waiting for you. The Goddess told me."

Fay never called the Moon Goddess Grace's mother. She only ever referred to her as the Goddess. Grace wondered if it was out of respect or possibly because saying it would remind Fay that Grace wasn't her child by blood. Either way, it didn't matter. As far as she was concerned, Fay was her mother. The only one she'd ever known. The only one she'd ever loved as a mother. Who had held her as a mother had. Wiped her tears as a mother should. Taught and raised her as only a mother would. Yes, in every way that mattered, Fay was Grace's mother, and that would never, ever change.

Grace scrunched up her face. "What is the Underworld? Is it a bar? A city?"

Fay shook her head. "The Underworld. Lucifer, Hades, Hel, The Underworld. You'll find an entrance in Los Angeles. The Goddess will guide you where you need to go. Follow her promptings. I did the best I could for you. She gave me a gift I never thought I would ever have. But your time has come. You have a destiny to fulfill. One that I knew would take you from me sooner or later. I wish…" She took in a ragged breath. "I just wish we had more time."

Grace fought to understand Fay's words. Underworld? Lucifer? Los Angeles? Destiny? She didn't understand.

"Go," said Fay. "Go now before I do. He will come as soon as I'm gone. This is the only way to keep you safe."

Grace shook her head. "Safe from who?"

The Alpha gold tinge overtook Fay's eyes, and though her alpha commands had never worked on Grace, she'd always respected what it meant. It meant business.

"I command you to go now. I command you to leave and seek out the Underworld. Don't stop until you get there. Until you are safe." Fay's voice came out stronger than it had in months. The wave of command pushed through Grace, and though it didn't compel her to do what her mother wanted, Grace knew that disobeying would disrespect the woman who had loved, raised, and protected her.

Tears flowed from Grace's eyes. "Please don't send me away yet," Grace whispered. "Please, Mom."

Tears flooded Fay's eyes, but the gold in her gaze blazed brighter.

Grace hugged her mom tight, remembering the wonderful times they'd shared. Learning to love reading. Learning to make wild berry jam from scratch. How to raise bees. How to hunt and run- even though she was never allowed to shift with the pack. Her love of old western movies. Nights looking up at the stars and talking about the stories of the Moon Goddess. Helping the pack. Playing with the pups. All of it. A beautiful life. A privileged life. And now it was ending. She was being sent away. Fay said it was for her own safety. Her destiny. But what destiny? And who was she being kept safe from? Shouldn't she be told?

Fay let go and pulled her hands away. "Go, Moon Child. Live your life. Find happiness."

Grace opened her mouth to speak, but no words came out.

The door behind them opened, and Old Robin walked in. Though a good twenty years older than her mother, Robin had always been her mother's best friend.

"Take her," Fay said.

Robin strode forward and lifted Grace to her feet. For only being five foot two and no more than a hundred pounds, Robin retained the strength of a wolf in their youth.

"Come," said Robin.

"But-" There was so much more Grace wanted to say, wanted to ask, needed to know… but she didn't get the chance. Robin ushered her out the door. Grabbed the two packed suitcases and nudged Grace to the back door with them.

Robin plopped the bags in the backseat of an old muscle car and opened the driver's side door for her

Grace looked back at the log cabin she'd grown up in.

Robin pulled her into a hug and then bent Grace's head to kiss it. "It has been an honor to know you, Goddess child."

Grace blinked. No one had ever called her that before, besides her mom. She hadn't even known Fay had told Robin. She'd made Grace swear not to tell anyone.

"Live well." Robin pulled a piece of paper from her pocket and pushed it into Grace's hand before helping Grace into the driver's seat, putting her seatbelt on her, and then closing the door.

"Go," said Robin. "Love and live."

Grace stared at Robin, wanting nothing more than to run back into the cabin to her mother. But she turned the car on instead. The engine roared to life, and she looked to the dirt drive heading away from the house. The road that would take her out of her woods. Out of her town. Out of her state. And into the unknown. She looked at the piece of paper in her hand, which read three words.

The Raven Weaver.

Dear Reader,

Thank you for taking the time to read *Loki's Warrior Mate.* I've been obsessed with mythology for as long as I can remember. The Norse Gods were always ones I wanted to write about, so I figured, why not give them their own series? I hope you enjoyed Loki and Val's story as much as I enjoyed writing it.

If you enjoyed the book, please take a moment to leave a review on your favorite retailer. Your reviews make all the difference to authors and to the success of books.

Feel free to take a moment to email me and let me know what you liked about the book, or who your favorite character was, and why. I love hearing from readers. It makes writing so much more fun when I hear from my readers.

VampWereZombie@Gmail.com

To find out more about me and my Upcoming Releases, Please Join my Street Team for Swag and Freebies.

I also love connecting with readers! Stalk me everywhere! I look forward to hearing from you!

Rebekah R. Ganiere - BOOKS WITH A BITE

USA Today Bestselling Author

Rebekah R. Ganiere

Dead Awakenings

Kissed by the Reaper

Fairelle Series

Red the Were Hunter - Book One

Yanti's Choice - Free Fairelle Short Story

Snow the Vampire Slayer - Book Two

Jamen's Yuletide Bride - Book Three

Zelle and the Tower - Book Four

Cinder the Fae - Book Five

Belle and the Beast - Book Six

Gerall's Festivus Bride - Book Seven

Jak the Giant Healer - Book Eight

Olivia and the Giant - Book Nine (April 2026)

Eric's Wayward Bride - Book Ten (Coming Soon)

Wolf River

PROMISED at the Moon

CURSED by the Moon

RECLAIMED from the Moon

TAMED under the Moon

UNLEASHED with the Moon

FATED despite the Moon

FOUND because of the Moon

ROCKED (2027)

The Society Series

Reign of the Vampires

Rise of the Fae

Vengeance of the Demons

Lycan King Wars

Alpha Marked

Alpha Claimed

Alpha Queen

Alpha King (2026)

Alpha Rogue (2026)

Tharnaxian Chronicles

The First

The Many (2027)

The Last (2027)

The Otherworlder Series

Kidnapped at Christmas

Vigilante at Valentine

Massacre at Mardi Gras

Hoodwinked at Halloween

Nightmare at New Year (2026)

Gods and Monsters Fated Mates

Thor's Feiry Mate

Loki's Warrior Mate

Fenrir Innocent Mate(2026)

Tyr Celestial Mate (2026)

Freya's Eternal Mates (2027)

Nocturne Bloodlines

Queen of the Night (2026)

Protector of the Night (2026)

Son of the Night (2027)

Immortal Monsters

Dracula's Bride

Frankenstein's Bride (Coming Soon)

Happy Holiday Romances

Rekindling Christmas

Christmas Lodge

NEWSLETTER

To claim your Two FREE Books and find out more about Rebekah R. Ganiere and her other Upcoming Releases You can Go Here:
www.RebekahGaniere.com/Newsletter

www.ingramcontent.com/pod-product-compliance
Lightning Source LLC
LaVergne TN
LVHW091121080826
845145LV00008B/1997

* 9 7 8 1 6 3 3 0 0 0 9 9 5 *